PRAISE FOR MICHAEL MELGAARD
AND *PALLBEARING*

"Michael Melgaard's stories are deceptively still on their surfaces, but just below run cross-currents of the darkest human emotions: fear, rage, and love. Melgaard's debut collection features characters in desperate situations, attempting to wrangle a drop of sense out of things while accepting or standing up to their fates. The stories in *Pallbearing* are crisp, ruefully funny, and unsentimental, each one a portrait on a grain of rice. A wonderful debut." —Michael Redhill, Scotiabank Giller Prize–winning author of *Bellevue Square*

"These powerful, empathetic stories are about the burdens people carry and the debts they owe — at work and at home, to their friends and family, and sometimes, heaviest of all, to themselves. With remarkable compression and insight, Michael Melgaard cuts straight to the heart of people's lives — in just a few pages I came to know these characters so well they felt like my own neighbours, and I'll remember them for a long time. This is a striking debut by a writer to watch." —Alix Ohlin, Scotiabank Giller Prize–shortlisted author of *Dual Citizens*

"With DNA traces of Raymond Carver and Kent Haruf, Michael Melgaard's *Pallbearing* conjures up a wallop of small-town pathos and dead-end desperation that will leave you shattered. These stories may be deceptively spare in their construction, but they are rich and abundant in their impact." —Michael Christie, Scotiabank Giller Prize–longlisted author of *Greenwood*

"Michael Melgaard does the hardest of things: the poetry of the everyday. Tough, heartbreaking, and astute, these stories move with grace through the margins of society, never condescending, never inauthentic. *Pallbearing* gives voice to the ignored, the invisible, the forgotten, and charges their lives with significance." —Tamas Dobozy, Rogers Writers' Trust Fiction Prize–winning author of *Siege 13*

"In spare, muscular prose, Melgaard illuminates the moments, big and small, that make us human. But don't be fooled by this deceptive simplicity — these stories will sneak up on you and knock the breath from your lungs. *Pallbearing* is a stunning debut." —Amy Jones, author of *Every Little Piece of Me*

"Each of the stories in *Pallbearing* is its own universe, orbiting around the exquisite edges of joy and sorrow. In prose at once searing and gentle, Michael Melgaard takes us through the infinitely tiny, infinitely vast moments that make up his characters' lives. In this collection, whole worlds live in the span of a gesture, a deep and riveting kind of magic." —Amanda Leduc, author of *The Miracles of Ordinary Men*

MICHAEL MELGAARD

PALLBEARING

STORIES

ASTORIA

Published in Canada in 2020 and the USA in 2020 by House of Anansi Press Inc.
www.houseofanansi.com

House of Anansi Press is committed to protecting our natural environment.
This book is made of made of material from well-managed FSC®-certified forests
and other controlled sources.

24 23 22 21 20   1 2 3 4 5

Library and Archives Canada Cataloguing in Publication

Title: Pallbearing : stories / Michael Melgaard.
Names: Melgaard, Michael, 1981– author.
Identifiers: Canadiana (print) 20190104376 | Canadiana (ebook) 20190104392 |
ISBN 9781487006150 (softcover) | ISBN 9781487006167 (EPUB) |
ISBN 9781487006174 (Kindle)
Classification: LCC PS8626.E4253 P35 2020 | DDC C813/.6—dc23

Library of Congress Control Number: 2019940909

Book design: Alysia Shewchuk

We acknowledge for their financial support of our publishing program the Canada
Council for the Arts, the Ontario Arts Council, and the Government of Canada.

Printed and bound in Canada

For Daniella

Contents

Pallbearing

Jonathan asked if this was where they should park. No one knew. It was a parking area with six spots just off the one-lane road that ran through the cemetery. They'd driven by three others like it, but this one was the first with a car in it. He slowed down and asked, "Do we know those people?"

Laura looked into the parked car and said, "I don't know. Maybe they were at the thing last night?" Anne and Matt agreed that they looked familiar.

"Good enough." Jonathan pulled in beside them.

He got out and tried to put the car keys in his pocket, which he found was sewn shut. The suit was new, bought after he'd been warned it would be needed, and he'd forgotten to pull out the tack stitching in the blazer, and, it turned out, in the pants too. He tried to pull open a pocket, but the stitching wouldn't give. He tried harder and it still held. He slipped the keys under the driver-side floor mat and took it on faith that people didn't steal cars at funerals.

Laura was talking to a woman from the other car. They were there for the same reason, but no one in that car knew where to go either. They all agreed it should be obvious, and everyone looked in different directions. The cemetery was all gentle rolling hills and little copses of trees — beautiful, but with no good sightlines. Anne pointed out that it was a natural burial, so probably not in the main graveyard; maybe somewhere near the back?

Jonathan saw a car driving slowly down a road on the other side of the graveyard. It stopped in one of the parking areas Jonathan had driven by. Laura was pretty sure that one of the people who got out was Rob. Jonathan squinted and agreed. They set out as a group across the grass, careful not to step on any graves. Jonathan wondered if he should introduce himself to the others, but he was pretty sure they'd met the night before; the details were hazy. Best to leave it.

It was Rob who had gotten out of the other car, but he'd been hoping Jonathan and his group knew where they were going. They talked it over and decided no one knew what to do, so they all just walked, spreading out across the cemetery, looking for something that would show them where they were supposed to be.

Just as Jonathan was starting to get nervous about them missing something, Laura pointed out a large group of people who appeared to be moving with purpose on the side of the cemetery they'd just come from. Jonathan's group, now scattered all over the manicured grass, turned around and headed back, converging on a path that led them over a wooded hill and down the other side where the trees gave way to a small open field bordered by a creek. Just along the tree line, there was a pile of dirt and a dark, rectangular hole.

Jonathan was surprised at how unprepared he was to see that hole. He looked away and tried not to think about how, in anywhere between five and thirty minutes, he would be carrying Alana there.

He collected himself and walked down the hill to join the others. No one was near the grave. They'd all stopped at the edge of the path and were milling around in small groups, waiting, Jonathan realized, for the arrival of the hearse. He didn't know what he was supposed to do — Alana's sister wasn't there and there was no one who looked like a funeral director. He stood near some people who weren't really talking and focused, instead, on the field itself.

What made this a natural graveyard, it seemed, was

a lack of lawn-mowing. Where the main cemetery had been tended to with golf course–like perfection, this was just a weedy lot with flattened grass paths to the more popular graves. Jonathan had been told that there were no fertilizers or chemicals on the ground, or in the ground. There had been no embalming, which is why the burial was rushed. Alana had died just the day before.

While Jonathan tried not to think about rates of decomposition, a light aqua-coloured van came over the hill, followed by two cars. The crowd cleared off the road to let it pass. The van stopped beside Jonathan, who saw through the tinted windows that there were no seats in the back, just a coffin. The sudden closeness of the body hit him. He looked away and wondered why the hearse was a light aqua-coloured van and not the usual black station wagon. He thought it might have something to do with it being a natural burial, but couldn't figure out how.

Alana's mother and sister got out of one of the cars, and another group — Jonathan thought they were maybe friends from her hometown — got out of the second. The driver of the van went over and talked to Alana's sister, who pointed at Jonathan. The driver walked back and offered Jonathan his hand with practised solemnity. He was, as it turned out, also the funeral director.

The other pallbearers realized their time was coming. They headed over to where Jonathan and the director stood behind the van, all of them shaking hands and nodding to each other. John was the only one Jonathan knew well; they'd been friends since before Jonathan had met Alana. Another was Alana's high-school boyfriend, who Jonathan remembered from the thing the night before. Two others were exes from before she got sick, and the last was someone she'd been seeing on and off for the last year or so. Mostly off, toward the end.

Nothing happened after the introductions were done. Jonathan figured they were waiting for stragglers. He looked at his watch, then thought that might be rude and turned the gesture into a stretch, which also seemed rude. He let his arms drop. No one was looking at him.

Jonathan wondered about the choice of pallbearers. All but John, he realized, had slept with Alana. She would have thought that was funny. Then he remembered that she had chosen the pallbearers herself, and that she would have had a chance to find it funny, and then he was holding back tears until he was cut off by the thought: Why only five of six?

He looked at John. He and Alana should not have had a chance to sleep with each other, since John had already been married when they met. But then,

Jonathan thought, maybe they had. It wasn't outside the realm of possibility for either of them. Or maybe Alana knew people would do the same math Jonathan had just done and wonder at the choice as well; maybe she had picked one person who she hadn't slept with just to mess with everyone. That was the sort of thing she would have found hilarious. Jonathan turned away and looked into the trees.

The funeral director called the pallbearers together. He gave them brief instructions that seemed obvious — they were to pick up the coffin and bring it to the grave. Then he opened the back door and it was all happening.

The coffin slid out. Jonathan was surprised by it. He'd been told it was going to be natural, which had made him imagine a rough-hewn, balsa wood apple crate or something. Instead, it was a plain, unvarnished coffin. There was no metal, just simple, well-made woodworked clasps and handles.

The coffin was at waist level. The proper grip to use hadn't been discussed. Jonathan started with overhand before he realized that would be awkward when he lifted, so switched to underhand. The pallbearers picked up the coffin. He waited for someone to give the word to lift it higher, but no one did and then they were moving. Jonathan thought they had missed a step. Didn't coffins normally go up on people's shoulders?

The coffin was awkward to carry. The weight threw off the pallbearers' balance, and their closeness to each other caused them to walk in a short shuffle step. Jonathan was surprised by the weight. It seemed heavy, at first, but a few steps later, he wondered if maybe it was actually lighter than it should be. The wood was, after all, quite dense. But by the end Alana had been so thin, something he then tried not to think about. He decided that he had no basis for comparison. There was no reason to think the coffin was either heavy or light; experientially, it was exactly the weight all coffins he had ever handled weighed.

Jonathan tried to counterbalance by throwing one arm out to the side, but then thought having one arm flapping might look disrespectful. Instead, he put it across his body and used it to help with the weight. The others struggled too. The natural burial field was riddled with little holes and clods of dirt. He wondered again why they hadn't lifted the coffin up on their shoulders. He was sure that's what they should have done, but it was too late to do anything about it now.

Then they were coming up on the hole. There were wide canvas straps across it, which were wrapped around a metal frame so the coffin could rest over the grave. The pallbearers walked on either side and stopped. A pallbearer opposite Jonathan shifted his grip, the coffin rocked, and when it stopped, something inside kept moving for a moment. Jonathan tried not to think about that while they lowered the coffin into place.

None of the pallbearers knew what to do now that their job was done. The ones on the far side walked around to the crowd that had followed them and now ringed the grave in a semicircle. Jonathan stepped back and then John shook his hand again for some reason. Behind, Jonathan could sense people shifting to see around him. He thought of walking farther back into the crowd, but then a woman Jonathan recognized as a friend of Alana's stepped forward and thanked everyone for coming. He thought she must be running the ceremony because then she talked about their shared experiences and the loss. Jonathan looked past her.

A creek cut through a field, then took a hard turn at the graveyard, separating it from what looked like a golf course on the other side. Jonathan turned his head away from the ceremony and saw a clubhouse. Definitely a golf course. He wondered at the creek's sudden turn; there must be some reinforcement to keep it from wearing into the dirt of the graveyard. The ground, he could see from the pile of dirt, was just sandy loam. It would only be a matter of time before the creek eroded the ground of the graveyard.

By then Alana would be part of the earth and would go out to the lake and then to sea. Jonathan figured that was the point of these organic burials—to return the body to nature. He felt tears coming again and focused on the woman running the ceremony.

She'd asked if anyone wanted to say a few words. There was a very long pause before Alana's high-school boyfriend stepped forward and told a story about how they'd met. After, a woman from Alana's book club read a children's story she said was a favourite of Alana's. Five pages in, Jonathan looked over the crowd. There were about forty people. Little groups of Alana's friends who weren't necessarily friends with each other. He tried to pick out who were people from high school and who were people from work or family.

Jonathan was thinking about how corny the story was and how there was no way Alana had a favourite kid's book when he realized that the woman had not only stopped talking but was now walking around the edge of the crowd handing out magic markers. The idea was for people to write messages on the coffin. There weren't enough markers to go around, so everyone would have to take turns. He watched a few people begin to write. Then a woman walked back from the coffin and held out a marker to him. Jonathan couldn't think of a way to say no that didn't make him seem like a monster, so he took the marker and immediately tried to pass it to John, who held up his hands and shook his head. Anne did the same.

By then there were no new message writers, so Jonathan tried to put the marker in his pocket. They were still stitched shut. Once again, he tried to rip open the pocket, but there was no give. He wondered what sort of fishing line the suit people had used. He clasped his hands behind his back and tried to listen to the woman running the ceremony but instead found himself reading what had been written on the coffin. There were X's and O's, some *I love you*'s, and a couple of *You were an inspiration and showed me how to live my life*'s. Jonathan thought again how corny it all was and then he was trying, again, not to cry.

A short silence followed, and then the funeral director asked the pallbearers to step forward. Jonathan was surprised to learn, just then, that they were now going to lower the coffin into the hole. At the last funeral he'd attended, this job had been done by a button attached to some sort of mechanical thing. But this was a natural funeral so he maybe should have expected an analog lowering, but he really wished someone had let him know in advance. Not that he would have said no; it just would have been nice to have been prepared.

And then he was at the grave and the funeral director was whispering instructions, explaining how they'd lower the canvas straps slowly and evenly as Alana went finally and definitively into the ground.

So, Jonathan thought, here goes. And then they were lifting the straps while the funeral director untied them from the anchors. Jonathan found the marker was still in his hand. He rolled it up between his thumb and index finger so it would be out of the way of the strap and then tried not to think that this weight, transferred from the body in the coffin up the canvas straps, was the last time he would have any human connection to Alana. The coffin lowered slowly into the ground.

It came to a rest on the dirt below. Under the guidance of the funeral director, the pallbearers on the far side let their straps down, and the pallbearers on Jonathan's side began to pull them up under the coffin.

Jonathan's strap was stuck. He wasn't sure what to do. If he pulled harder, he worried that whatever it was caught on wouldn't unstick and instead pull the coffin onto its side. He briefly had a vision of the coffin flipping open and everyone screaming and horrified, and him trying to explain that it wasn't his fault that this was a stupid hippie funeral with no button to lower the coffin and that he had no idea he had to do anything but show up and everyone would think he was the biggest asshole in the world and never talk to him again.

Jonathan looked up at the funeral director. "It's stuck," he explained.

The funeral director went behind Jonathan and reached his arms around either side of him to grab the strap. They pulled together and the coffin shifted slightly, but the strap came free. Jonathan quickly rolled it up.

He blushed and stepped back into the crowd and tried to make himself small. The woman running things smiled at him before she started talking again. He wondered what other surprise pallbearer duties were left. There was still that pile of dirt. Did they expect him to fill in the grave? He didn't see any shovels, but they could be in the van or a nearby shed. Was the funeral director on his way to get them? Jonathan turned his head slightly. The funeral director was standing just outside the circle of mourners. No shovels in sight.

The book club lady was doing something again. She and a few of the others walked through the crowd handing out flowers. They were tulips; Jonathan ended up with four of them. The book club lady was explaining that they had been Alana's favourite flower. That was news to him; it had never occurred to him that Alana would have a favourite flower.

There was more talking, about how this was not a goodbye and Alana living on in memory. They shared a long moment of silence. Then the woman in charge of the ceremony said a few more words about the community of support. She ended by telling everyone to take all the time they needed.

A few people from Alana's work dropped their flowers into the grave and Jonathan understood they weren't for keeping. Others stepped forward, some bowed their heads before adding their flowers, others turned right back into the crowd after. Jonathan waited for an appropriate moment and then tossed his flowers into the hole. There was a clunking noise. He peered into the grave and saw his magic marker lying with the flowers on top of the plain wooden coffin covered with well wishes. He stepped back.

And then he turned into the crowd. Anne and Laura both hugged him and John shook his hand again. Jonathan kept moving past them and through the others until he was out of the crowd and crossing the open field. He walked to the edge of the creek and breathed in deeply. He looked down and saw that the creek bank was, indeed, reinforced against erosion—concrete slabs held in place with wire mesh. Jonathan wondered how long that sort of thing would hold, and then he let himself cry.

Fun Centre

[1]

Charles walked around to the back of the giant ice cream cone and ducked inside its tiny door. He turned on the register and pulled the float out of the tin can he kept hidden in one of the empty ice cream pails. Then he slid the serving window open and sat down with his book.

Greg yelled at him from the go-kart track across the parking lot. Charles waved out the window and went back to reading. When he looked up, Greg was standing at the window. He said, "Those fuckers say I'm greasing up their shitter. They don't want me using their can no more." Charles marked his place with a finger. "They want me to get porta potties to put by the track. You know how fucking much that will cost?" Charles made a noise that he hoped sounded like commiseration. "They treat me like a fucking second-class citizen. We all work together here to help each other, man. My karts bring in business for their fucking putt–putt. It's fucking synergy. Fuck man, this is the shits." Greg looked up at the menu and said, "Give me an ice cream sandwich, eh?"

"I keep telling you, you can pay cost, but I can't give it to you for free. It's a buck fifty."

"I don't take nothing for free, man. I told you, you can use the karts anytime."

"I own a car. If I feel like driving, I will do it in my car, that I am the owner of."

"Fuck you, man." Greg fished some change out of his pockets and slapped it down on the counter. He walked back across the parking lot, giving the finger to the Fun Centre on his way by. Charles put the change in the till and went back to his book.

[2]

Charles watched a man who looked to be pushing a hundred finish the par-three course and pull a cart full of clubs to the back of his car. He left them there and came over to Charles's window. He said, "You weren't open earlier."

"Oh, no, sorry. There's not much call for ice cream before noon."

"I would have bought one. It's a shame you don't open earlier."

"Can I get you one now?"

"It's too late for ice cream."

"That's funny. Most people like to have their ice cream after lunch."

"I like to have something sweet *before* lunch."

They stared at each other.

"I'd like a hot dog now."

"Sorry, I just have ice cream."

"I know that. I'm going to go get a hot dog in town."

Charles watched the old guy shuffle back to his car and struggle to get his golf bag into the trunk. He rolled it in, eventually, and then stretched up to close the trunk. He got in the car and nothing happened for a long time. Charles was about to go check on him when the engine fired up. The car made a beeping noise as it backed up.

[3]

A car pulled into the parking lot and a woman got out and set up some balloons on one of Charles's picnic tables. Other cars and a van came in and then a dozen adults and twice as many kids were running around. Someone took out a cooler and a bunch of two-litre bottles of soda. One of the moms said, "Oh fuck," and looked around. She walked up to Charles's window. "You got any plastic cups?"

"No, but I sell soda."

"We got our own, we just need cups."

"Sorry, can't help you."

She went back to Charles's tables and said, "He didn't have none." One of the dads drove off and came back a few minutes later with cups. Then the kids split up. Some went to the putt-putt, the others to the go-karts. They left all their coolers and food on the tables. When they were done, they came back and had sandwiches out of the cooler and chips and more soda and then a cake with candles and sparklers. One of the kids asked for ice cream.

A dad approached the window. "Hey, give me a couple drumsticks and a couple those ice cream sandwiches." Charles pulled them out of the freezer and rang it up. The guy said, "Jesus. Three bucks each?" Charles shrugged and the guy said, "You can do better than that. They're like a buck at the corner store."

"Sorry, that's the price."

"But I'm buying four."

Charles held out his hands. The guy paid and went

back to the tables. Charles heard him say "rip-off," and his wife said something that ended with "asshole." They all piled back into their cars and took off. Charles ducked out the back door and threw their garbage into the trash can.

[4]

Greg came over. "You see that one lady with the birthday party?"

"Probably."

"She was into me. I seen her at the bar last week. She recognized me."

"That's great."

"I should have got her number."

"I thought you didn't date women with kids?"

"Who said anything about dating?"

"Right. So, how're you going to see her again?"

"I'll look her up in the phone book. She told me her name was Linda, and one of the kids called her Mrs. McAlister."

"Mrs.?"

"Fuck, they keep their husband's name sometimes."

"But you don't know?"

"If a guy picks up, I'll hang up."

"Solid plan."

"Fuck you, man."

[5]

It got busy. Charles tucked his book under the register and scooped ice cream. Greg was busy digging
go-karts out of the tire walls, and a line had formed
at the first hole of the putt-putt. Charles ran out of
Rocky Road. He locked up the till and ran over to the
Fun Centre basement where he kept his extra stock
in a couple of deep freezes. The owner's son, Randy,
was down there with his buddy, who also worked at
the Fun Centre. They were both high. Randy said,
"Hey, Ice Cream Man."

Charles asked him what was up. Before Randy
could answer, his dad shouted for them to get the
fuck back to work from the top of the stairs. Randy
laughed, but his buddy at least looked like he thought
he should do something. Then Randy's dad was down
there and told them to get the fuck out on the driving
range and pick up the balls. Randy made a joke about
picking up his balls that was a little too loud. His
dad heard and started laying into them about fucking
around and how he had a good mind to whoop both
of them. The shouting got quieter as they got farther
away, but the last thing Charles heard was ". . . end up
like the ice cream guy." Charles slammed the deep
freeze and headed back across the parking lot.

[6]

"Hey Charles, you still work here?"

"Yeah, well, I bought it a few years ago, so I'm the owner now..."

"That's cool. You're like your own boss. Must make money?"

"I do okay. Can I get you something..." And then it came to him: "Chet?"

"Yeah, I'll take three double cones, one peppermint, one chocolate, and my little boy wants that tiger stripe shit."

Charles bent down into the freezer and scooped out the ice cream. He handed the first cone over the counter. Chet passed it down to his kid and asked, "So, you still playing in those bands?"

"Here and there."

"Cool. Doing any records?"

"We record sometimes."

"You ever on the radio or anything?"

"We're not really a commercial band."

"Oh, cool. Like, indie stuff?"

"Sure. I didn't know you had a kid."

"Yeah, this is Chad. Three years old now. Thank the ice cream man, Chad."

Chad stared up at Charles. Charles smiled and waved. Chet said "just a second" and went down to the picnic table where a large woman swung a purse over her belly and fished around for money.

"So, who's the wife?" Charles asked when he got back.

"What do you mean? That's Barb."

"*That's* Barb?"

"Hey, fuck you man."

"No, I didn't mean it like that. It's just I haven't seen her in a while."

"Yeah, well you're probably pulling in prime pussy with your fucking ice cream shack."

"I didn't mean —"

Chet grabbed Chad's arm and pulled him away. Charles watched them get into their car and leave. He went back to his book.

[7]

Charles heard banging behind the ice cream shack. He opened the little back door and saw a kid on the putt-putt course hitting one of the fibreglass animals, a deer, with a club. Charles walked up to the fence that separated the parking lot from the course. He said, "You probably shouldn't be doing that." The kid looked up. He was red in the face, freckled, and sweaty. He swung his club around and let it go. It landed in one of the flower beds. The kid walked away.

[8]

Things slowed down around six. Charles sat at one of his picnic tables and ate a sandwich while he read. A group of teenage girls were playing putt-putt. Charles watched over the top of his book as one of them bent down to pull a ball out of the hole. She stood up and made eye contact with Charles; he looked back at the page. Charles heard some whispering and they all started giggling. He glanced up when they were at the next hole and one of them was crouched down with her back to him. Another one of them leaned over her golf club stretching and smiled when she saw that he was watching. He nodded and tried to go back to his book. They went around the course like that, stretching and bending and smiling. One of them waved and he thought maybe one of them blew him a kiss. They giggled a lot.

When they went into the Fun Centre to return their putters, Charles went around back and ducked into his ice cream cone. Two of the girls came up to the window. One of them asked what sort of ice cream he had.

"The usual, Rocky Road, mint, vanilla..."

"How much?"

"Two dollars a scoop."

She stuck a hand in her pocket. Her fingers wiggled

where the pocket stuck out the bottom of her cut-offs. She said, "I only have a dollar. Do you think maybe that would be okay?"

Charles guessed it could be.

The other girl asked Charles his name. She said she really wanted some ice cream, Charles, but didn't have any money. He handed them both a cone and then watched them walk back to the others. They all started giggling again and he heard one of them say, "You slut," to the one in the short-shorts.

They got in their car and left. Across the parking lot, Greg grabbed his crotch and shouted something that Charles didn't try to make out.

[9]

It was getting late and a bunch of guys in their late teens were drinking beer on one of Charles's picnic tables. They'd finished up a round of putt-putt and tried to go on the go-karts. Greg hadn't let them, and now they were sitting around talking loudly about what a "faggot skid" the go-kart guy was. After a bit, Charles said, "Come on guys, there's kids around."

They all looked at him. One of them said, "You *wish* there were kids around." They laughed and high-fived.

Charles shook his head and went back to his book.

The guy who had talked came up to the window. He wasn't wearing a shirt and was surprisingly ripped. He said, "So, did you go to ice cream school to get this job."

Charles put down his book. "It was ice cream university, and I did a post-grad."

"Is that why you think you can tell me what to do, ice cream fag?"

"That's Dr. Ice Cream Fag. And, look, there's like nine cameras in this parking lot recording what's going on. I presume one of you is going to drive, and I'm almost positive none of you are sober. On top of which, you're maybe seventeen at the oldest. It would take me literally three seconds to ruin your night, so you should just get the fuck out of here."

The kid started to look around for the cameras. Charles picked up his phone and made as if he were dialing. The kid said, "You fucking rat."

Charles smiled and said into the phone, "Hello, the police?" The kid told his friends they needed to get the fuck out of there. They peeled out of the parking lot. Charles waved goodbye.

[10]

Charles waited for the last family to finish at the putt-putt. When they left without buying anything, he closed up. He printed out the day's receipts, noted the amounts in his book, and put a deposit in an envelope. The float went back into the tin and then into one of the empty ice cream pails. He slid the window shut and ducked out the back door and padlocked it behind him.

He got into his van. Greg was working on one of his karts and stood up and shouted for Charles to hold on a second. Charles waved out the window and pulled out of the parking lot and onto the highway.

A Pregnancy

Three months into the pregnancy, two weeks after Ryan and Julie found out they were having twins and a week before they planned to let everyone know, they were told that one of the fetuses was not viable. Julie asked the doctor what that meant. He said the organs were not forming correctly — the baby, a girl, would not make it to term.

He went on, explaining to Ryan that there was a chance the non-viable fetus's continued development might affect the other twin — a boy who appeared to be developing without complication. Though, the doctor was quick to add, they still needed to perform more tests to be sure. He said it might become necessary to terminate the non-viable fetus to protect the other — Julie's shoulder tensed under Ryan's hand when the doctor said "terminate"—and that they would have to monitor the situation closely. He told them their pregnancy was now considered high-risk. They would need to come for a checkup every week, and if there was any abdominal pain, no matter how slight, they were to head straight to the emergency. He asked if they had any questions.

Julie waited until they were in the car before she said, "That horrible doctor didn't even look at me." She said she hated that he called her little baby a fetus, and that he obviously didn't care at all about anyone's feelings. She asked why someone like that would even become a doctor. Ryan told her it was normal for doctors to be like that; they were trained to keep their distance. Julie asked why he was defending that horrible man and Ryan said he wasn't defending him, just explaining, and then they both stopped talking.

Julie went straight to the bathroom when they got home. She got in the shower and turned her face into the water and watched it flow down her chest and over her still-flat belly and thought about the two lives inside it and how one of them was not viable. Later, Ryan let himself in. Julie sat on the edge of the tub. He sat beside her and put an arm over her shoulder and pulled her close. She turned her face into his chest and said, "Our little girl is going to die."

They went to see the doctor every week. Julie kept

quiet while the doctor went over test results with Ryan and told them the same things about being careful and taking care of themselves. She was quiet on the rides home and quiet all the days and nights in between. Ryan didn't know what else to do, so he ended up being quiet beside her. They went to work and watched TV and ate their meals and sometimes Julie would talk about it on the phone with her mom, but mostly she kept to herself. They tried to go shopping for baby things once, but at the store Julie said she couldn't do it; she couldn't not buy clothes for the girl who was still alive but wouldn't be. They went back home.

A week before her third trimester, a stomach pain woke Julie in the middle of the night. Ryan wanted to go to the hospital right away, but she said it was probably nothing and they should wait and see if it happened again. Then she felt something under the covers and reached down and her hand came up covered in blood. Ryan hurried her into the car and to the emergency. She was taken away on a gurney while he found a place to park. When he finally got inside, Julie was gone and a nurse led him to a waiting room and told him they would let him know as soon as they had news.

A doctor Ryan had never met came in and told Ryan the non-viable fetus had died. That had caused

Julie to go into labour—her body was rejecting the dead fetus, but in the process, it was rejecting the healthy one as well. They had given her drugs to stop the labour and they could hold it off for a while, but there was only so much they could do to prevent it entirely. If their still-living baby was to have any chance of survival, it would need, at the very least, another week in the womb. More time would be better.

Ryan brought some things from home—blankets and clothes and their tablet to watch movies—and moved into the chair in Julie's hospital room. He called her work and explained about the early maternity leave and he called his work and said he might not be in for a while. That first day they put a needle through Julie's belly and injected the baby with steroids to help the lungs develop. She was given pills that kept her tired and nauseous all day. In the middle of the first night she asked Ryan if he thought their baby knew his sister had died. Then she said she could hold on, that she had to. Every night before she fell asleep she would count down the days they needed to be sure the baby would be okay, saying, just six more, then five, then four.

Three days before the doctor's deadline, Julie woke up with a stomach pain that quickly got worse. While the nurses pushed her bed through the hospital she kept saying, "No, it's too soon, please God no." Ryan caught the elbow of their doctor and asked him if it had been long enough; he told Ryan they'd do everything they could.

The labour lasted into the early morning. Julie stopped screaming and just numbly pushed toward the end. Ryan was trying to bring her back to the world, holding her hand and saying it would be okay when the first baby came out. Julie asked, "Which?" but it was taken away and then she had to push out the second and then the placenta. Ryan only glanced at the babies; he stayed with Julie while they were taken away.

Later, the doctor told Ryan it had gone as well as could be expected—their boy was alive, but his heartbeat was weak and he was on a ventilator and would be for a long time. The doctor was very careful to say there was still a long road ahead of them. The baby would need surgery soon and there would be a lot of things to overcome before they could be sure the child would survive. Then he shook Ryan's hand and offered his congratulations.

By the next evening, Julie was recovered enough to see their child. Ryan helped her into a wheelchair the hospital required her to use, and then a nurse led them to the neonatal ICU—she told them it was called the "miracle ward," because they'd seen so many there.

There were two rows of incubators. The nurse led them to the one second from the end and said, "Here's your brave little guy."

When Ryan was young he had knocked a bird's nest out of a tree with a slingshot. The eggs cracked open on the ground and he had watched as the half-formed chicks, purple, slimy, and barely recognizable as birds, struggled and then died. His son looked like one of those birds—too small, too new. His skin was translucent, covered with yellow and purple blotches that Ryan realized were organs moving under the skin. There were needles and tubes taped into the arms and stomach; a too-large ventilator came out of the baby's mouth. It looked like it was choking him. It looked horrible.

Julie said, "Oh my God, our poor little guy," and put a hand on the plastic shell between them. She said, "Look at how small his fingers are," and Ryan watched the tiny pink hand move from side to side and Julie said that he was trying to wave.

All Ryan could say was, "It's so premature."

Julie looked up at him and said, "*Jeremy* is so premature, and of course he is." And she said this would be hard for them, but it was harder for him and they had to be there for their little boy and give him strength. And Ryan started to say something that got caught up by tears and then Julie was comforting him.

She told him it would be all right and after a while Ryan said that Jeremy was going to make it, he had to.

Julie asked the nurse if she could hold him. She said she was sorry, but the risk of infection was too great. Then she smiled and told them that in a couple of weeks little Jeremy would be allowed out and he would be big and strong like his dad and they could hold him and play with him all they wanted. Julie and Ryan smiled back. Julie put her hand on the plastic again and said goodbye and good luck and that they loved him and would see him soon. As the nurse led them out she said, "Aren't they just the most precious things."

That night Julie and Ryan were woken by a doctor and told that Jeremy needed surgery immediately. They moved into a waiting room and a few minutes later another doctor they didn't know came in and explained that they had done everything they could, but it had just been too soon. Ryan nodded and thanked him and said he knew they had tried their best. Julie said if only she could have held on a couple more days, and Ryan told her not to think like that—there was nothing any of them could have done differently. Then the doctor was gone and later a nurse came into their room and asked if they'd like to see Jeremy.

They were led through the hospital together,

through a room with curtains drawn around beds and then into a smaller one. Jeremy lay in the middle of a too-large bed, a blanket pulled up to his neck. The tubes and wires and ventilator were all gone. He looked, for the first time, like a baby. Julie stood back and held on to Ryan and then she bent close to the bed and pulled the blanket back before the nurse could tell her not to. There were large black stitches across his chest. She didn't look at that, but lifted him up cupped in her two hands. She held him against her chest and kissed his forehead. Ryan held her shoulders and touched the side of his child's cold face.

Then Julie asked where their little girl was. The nurse hesitated and said it might be difficult and Julie said she would like to see her, please. The nurse said if they were sure and when Julie only stared back, she left. She came back pushing another large bed with an even smaller body on it. The nurse told Ryan they really should leave the blanket on and Julie crouched down beside the tiny face and reached out her hand. Ryan touched her shoulder and started to say no, but Julie just put a finger on the baby's face. Then she pulled Ryan's hand down to do the same. She said, "Isabel, can we call her Isabel?" Ryan said of course; it was a pretty name.

They had a small ceremony for the twins at the hospital chapel before Julie checked out. It was just the two of them and a priest. Ryan told everyone but their closest family that Julie had miscarried and that they didn't want any cards or anything like that. Back at home, they set about recovering. Ryan went back to work; Julie did not. She asked her job to change the maternity leave to extended sick leave, and when that was up, a leave of absence. She spent her days in bed or on the couch. Their family doctor prescribed antidepressants that she never took. Her mother visited every day and her friends came on weekends but she didn't like them to stay long. Not much changed for the first few months. They were exhausted, emotional. And then things got hard. They had a few fights and then a blowout that ended with Julie moving into her mom's house for two weeks.

After that, it got a little better. They started going for walks and then into town to run errands together. They went for drives on the weekend. There were still things that set her off—babies in carriages, pregnant women—but it got so they could work through the worst days. Eventually they went out with friends and she drank too much the first few times and Ryan had to get her home while she cried and screamed and then that stopped too. By then it had been a year.

She started work, part-time at first. They went on a short vacation. They got past the feeling of just sticking things out and started to feel love for each other again. They were closer than before, the marriage stronger. They never talked about trying to have another child, but when Julie got pregnant again, she simply told Ryan that she was going to go through with it. Julie's pregnancy went smoothly. A year later they were expecting another.

The pain still came out sometimes. Like one night when the whole family was over for dinner and her mother-in-law asked if Julie was excited to have a second child. Julie said that it was her fourth, and she said it with all the force of her loss. Everyone stopped eating and looked anywhere but at her until her mother-in-law said yes, of course. A minute later Julie excused herself. Ryan followed her into the kitchen where she was crying over the sink and saying, they were real, I touched them, they were real. And Ryan held on to her and said that he knew, he had held them too.

Rob and Jane

Upstairs, something with wheels ran back and forth along the floor and then it sounded like something heavy fell over. Rob heard one of the boys say "Oh-oooo," and then the house was quiet. He buried his head under the couch cushion and fell back asleep.

A little later he woke up to warm heavy breathing by his ear. He pushed the dog away and told it to fuck off. It licked his hand. He pulled the pillow off his head and saw Billy standing there. Billy said, "Dad, can I watch cartoons?"

"Sure. Just not too loud, okay?"

"Thanks, Dad."

"But get me a glass of water first."

Billy said, "Okay, sure," and ran out of the room, sliding on his socks around the corner. He came back with a glass of water filled right to the brim, held at arm's length in front of him. He walked carefully toward Rob, spilling only a little, and put the glass down on the coffee table and then turned on the TV, scooting up close to the screen.

Jack had followed his brother as far as the doorway. He stood, half hidden by the wall, staring at his dad. Rob waved at him. Jack walked across the living room, still staring at his dad. When he got to where his brother was, he lowered himself onto his knees, and then, finally, turned away from his dad so he could watch the show. Rob shook his head and sat up to drink.

Rob watched the cartoons for a couple of minutes before his hangover sent him to the bathroom. He stuck his head under the tap and drank and then settled onto the toilet and flipped through an old *National Geographic*. There was a story on the world's deepest lake he'd read dozens of times before, but the pictures of the impossibly thick ice and the wild, barren shores were always nice to look at. He thought about what it would be like to live there, isolated in the deep snow for months of the year. He could learn to fish, to live off the land.

When Rob opened the door Billy was standing right there. He said, "Stinky Daddy!" and put both palms over his mouth to make a farting noise. Then he squeezed between Rob and the sink and climbed up onto the toilet. Billy sang a song about pooping. Rob left him to it.

In the kitchen, Rob dumped the old coffee grounds into the garbage and pulled up the sides of the bag so it wouldn't spill over. He filled up the percolator and looked around for the coffee. An empty tin sat beside the garbage. He heard Jane tell Jack not to sit so close to the TV and then she came into the kitchen. She dropped Lily into the jumper.

"Where'd you end up last night?"

"Matty's."

"You go out?"

"We had one at the Oak."

"We can't afford that."

"Matty bought."

"Are you sure?"

Rob went out to the porch and pulled a pack of cigarettes off the window sill. He sat on the old armchair they kept out there and read the newspaper that had been leaning against their door. A neighbour pushed his lawnmower up and down his yard, filling the air with the smell of exhaust and fresh-cut grass. Rob smoked his cigarette and then sank down into the chair and closed his eyes. The lawnmower stopped. He heard a garage door close and then it was quiet except for the sound of the grass righting itself.

• • •

ROB WOKE UP TO the dog nuzzling into his crotch. The neighbour was watering his lawn; Rob figured he must have been out only a minute.

Inside, the boys were sitting on chairs pulled up close to the kitchen table, shovelling cereal toward their mouths. Their chins were dripping milk and a line of spilt food led back to their bowls. Rob bounced the springs of Lily's jumper to get her going and she laughed and clapped and dropped her sippy cup. He left her bouncing and took a drink of Billy's juice.

"Daaad!"

"Hey, don't worry about it."

Jack stared at his dad and pulled his glass toward him. He lowered it onto the floor. Then he covered his cereal with both arms and leaned over it.

Rob looked in the cupboard for a glass but could only find a measuring cup. He filled that up with juice and tore a bagel out of the bag. He slathered cream cheese on it. Jane came in wrapped in a towel, still dripping from the shower. She picked up Lily's sippy cup and looked at Rob.

"What?"

"You couldn't clean a glass?"

"I didn't want to use the water while you were in the shower."

"Well, I'm out now."

Rob put the bagel in his mouth, collected his juice,

and went back to the living room. A little later Jane came in, now wearing a T-shirt and jeans. She tilted her head to one side and wrung the water out of her hair. She said she was going to pick up the mail and do some shopping; she'd be back in a bit. Rob said, "Pick me up a coffee, would you? We're out."

The boys sat back in front of the TV after Jane left. Rob told them to keep an eye on their sister and went up to the bathroom. He shaved, took a couple painkillers, and turned on the shower. Billy banged on the door and said he had to go potty. Rob said to go in the basement, which Billy told him was too scary. Rob said, "Figure it out," and turned his face into the water pouring down from above. He let it wash over him for a good long time.

Jane got home just as he was coming down the stairs. She had grocery bags hanging from both wrists, a coffee in one hand, and the mail in the other. "Give me a hand with this," she said.

Rob took the coffee and mail. Jane said, "I didn't see the cheque." He followed her into the kitchen where she dumped the groceries onto the kitchen table and started separating meat into freezer bags. Rob put the cereal into the cupboards above her head and then the cans of soup into the pantry on the other side of her. When he asked her to move over so he could put the cleaning stuff under the sink she told him he was more in the way than anything else and she could handle unpacking. He grabbed a package of crackers and his coffee and went back to the living room.

A little later Jane shouted for the boys to turn off the TV and get out of their pyjamas for the day. Billy looked back at his dad. Rob said, "Do what your mother says." Billy ran off and Jack backed out slowly, staring. Jane came in and put Lily in the playpen and asked Rob what his plans were for rest of the day. He said he was going to head into town that afternoon. She said there was a pile of library books by the door that had to go back.

He went upstairs and lay down on the bed. When he woke up, it was mid-afternoon. The kids were out back playing with Jane. He looked in Jane's purse for bus fare, but she didn't have any cash. Instead, he pulled a bunch of DVDs off the shelf over the TV. He shouted "bye" out the back door and headed into town.

ROB PUT HIS BACKPACK down on the counter. The guy who ran the pawnshop looked up at him and then went back to tidying the display case. After a few minutes he went into the back, leaving Rob alone to look over the display of swords. He wondered how long it would take to get good with a sword, and thought of various situations where that would be useful. Then he wondered why so many swords were getting pawned. Was there a down-on-his-luck samurai in town? Who actually bought these things?

The guy came back out and said, "You got to take them out of the bag."

Rob unzipped his backpack and piled up the DVDs. The guy went through them. Every once in a while he'd pop open a case and look at the disc. When he was done, he held up the five he'd separated and said, "I can do ten for these. Can't use the others."

"What about forty for everything?" Rob said.

The guy laughed. "I don't want those. At all. Even the ones I'm taking, I barely want. They're all scratched, the cases are covered in juice or some shit."

"Thirty?"

"Ten for those. Take the rest home with you."

"There's, like, twenty DVDs there. Twenty?"

"I can do twenty." The guy popped open the till and handed Rob a bill.

ROB SAT AT A table in the middle of the empty bar and worked his way through a burger and a beer. A nature show played on the TV. Some sort of African deer looked up, startled, and then resumed licking the surface of a river. The show cut to a shot of a lion loping across a plain, then back to the deer. The narrator let Rob know that the lion had some competition and would not be getting his meal that day. A crocodile jumped out of the water and pulled the deer in. "Jesus," Rob said to no one.

Matty walked in and said "Hey." He switched the TV over to the sports channel and sat down. Sawdust floated off his shoulders. He shouted an order at the waitress. The sports channel had no sport on, just a countdown show with the week's most outrageous moments. They watched together without talking much. Number one was two hockey goalies fighting. Then the baseball pregame show started. Matty's burger arrived. When they had emptied their first beers, Rob said, "Let me get us a pitcher."

Matty said, "You got the money you owe me?"

"Not yet. But I got some. I'll buy."

"I'll take it."

Rob took their plates up to the counter and ordered a pitcher. Back at the table, Matty took a sip and said, "What the fuck is this?"

"What do you mean? It's beer."

"No, I mean what kind of beer. It tastes like piss."

"It's the special."

"You cheap asshole. Tell me next time and I'll float you the extra dollar so we don't have to drink beer that gives me the shits."

Matty lit a smoke and took a couple drags. Rob tried not to look until Matty muttered something and slid the pack across the table. Rob asked, "Can I have your light?"

"What a guy you are."

They watched the game and played pool. Matty picked up another pitcher of "the good stuff"; it was empty by the fifth inning. Matty went for a piss and Rob fed his last quarter into the pull tab machine. He didn't win. The empty pitcher sat there until the bottom of the sixth when the waitress came around and asked if they were getting another. Matty looked at Rob, who leaned back and patted his pockets and said it was maybe time he got going.

"Ah, fuck it. I'll buy. But you owe me."

"I'm good for it."

"You gotta be good for something."

The place started to fill up. Some of the boys Matty worked with joined them and a couple old friends sat at another table. A group of guys they knew from around showed up after their football game. It turned out to be a friend of a friend's birthday and the party started picking up around eight. Someone bought a round of shots that Rob got in on and then he helped himself to a top-up from a pitcher. After a bit he bummed a quarter from Matty to call home.

"You forgot the library books."

"I ran into some of the boys. I'll be home in a bit."

"I won't wait up."

"I won't be that long."

"Did you take some DVDs?"

"Huh? I lent Matty a couple."

"You lent Matty *The Lion King*?"

"No. *Die Hard*."

"There's a bunch of others missing."

"Maybe the kids moved them."

"Sleep in the bed tonight, huh? I don't like the kids waking up to their father passed out on the couch."

"I'll see you soon."

ROB WALKED THROUGH THE dark between street-lamps. He was climbing the hill home, sweating and smoking the last cigarette he'd bummed from Matty. He crossed through a pool of light and focused on the next. At the top he caught his breath and looked back. The streetlights bent with the road and back into town. Nothing stayed open late downtown; the only light came from the grid of streetlights and the big gas station sign out on the highway. He watched a car turn onto the highway and drive out of town, disappearing over the bridge, the lights blocked by the woods. He turned around and kept going.

He focused and leaned toward the next light and

then the next and then there wasn't another until the corner of his subdivision. For a long time it didn't seem to be getting any closer and then he was crossing under it and looking at the bank of mailboxes. He didn't have the key with him, and anyways he was sure Jane had checked earlier.

Rob cut through the schoolyard. He sat down on the edge of a slide and patted his pockets, looking for a smoke to have before he got home. He couldn't find one but sat there for a few minutes, staring at the dark windows of the houses that backed on to the school. No one moved in any of the houses.

He cut through one of the yards to get back to his street. All the lights were out at home. He put the key in the lock and pushed the door open. The dog was standing there wagging its tail. It whined and Rob shushed it. He went up to the bathroom and took a piss, sitting down so he didn't make any noise.

He looked in on Lily sleeping. She wheezed and he left quietly. In the boys' room, Jack had climbed up to Billy's bunk and they had kicked the blanket off onto the floor. They both looked blue from the nightlight. Rob pulled the blanket up over them. He bumped into the doorjamb hard on the way out. One of the boys rolled over, but didn't wake up.

Jane said hi when he got into their room. He sat on the edge of the bed and pulled off his pants. She said that he smelled like cigarettes and onions and asked what time it was. Rob said it wasn't that late and that he needed some water and would be back in a minute.

He went down to the couch and lay down to sleep.

Coming and Going

Barb would sometimes almost miss a car coming or going. There were things that dragged her away from her station at the window, of course — dishes, laundry, cooking, sleep — but over the years she'd found ways to work around the distractions. Dishes were done at night, when the light from the cars shining into the living room let her know someone was there. A service handled her laundry. Her food was almost all pre-made, microwaveable. And she'd started sleeping on the couch across from the window so the lights would wake her up. But the runs into town to get groceries and fill her prescriptions weren't easily handed off.

She'd managed to get them down to one hour-long trip every two weeks — on Wednesday nights at eight, which she'd worked out was the time she was least likely to miss any action—but even that ended up being too much time away. Eventually, Barb was forced to get back in touch with her son. Claiming a bad back, she asked if he could help her out from time to time.

MARK ALWAYS SURPRISED HER by being old and overweight and bald. In her mind, he was still a gawky teenager. But now he showed up every Sunday, sweating over the grocery bags as he backed in through the trailer door. The first time he'd come, she'd thought it was her ex-husband. That impression stuck.

"Here's your groceries, Ma." Mark dropped the bags on the kitchen table and went straight to the sink to pour himself a glass of water. Sweat stains grew under his arms and spotted down his back; she could practically see them spreading, like a toddler peeing his pants.

He gulped down the water and let out a sigh that she could hear across the trailer. "Did you get to the doctor about your back?"

"I don't need a doctor to tell me to stay off my feet." A car turned into view, a neighbour. She didn't bother marking it down in her book.

"Yeah, Ma, but maybe you can get it straightened

or something. Janice, down at work, she saw an acupuncturist. Fixed her right up."

"There's that Janice you always talk about. Have you asked her out yet?"

"No, Ma. She remains married."

"You'd find a girl if you lost a little weight. Women don't mind bald men as much as they used to. It's fashionable now."

"Ma, come on." His hands went up to his head to straighten hair that wasn't there, a habit he shared with his father. She could never figure out why it was that his dad never had any trouble finding women, but her son remained single.

He came into the living room and sat down on the couch, sighing again. He lifted one leg to pull the blanket out from under him. "Do you sleep out here?"

"It's good for my back."

"Doesn't the light bother you? I could help you move the couch under the window, then at least you wouldn't get it right on your eyes."

"It doesn't bother me." He looked past her, out the window. Another car came in; she glanced and wrote down the first few digits of the licence plate.

"What're you writing there?" He got up to look.

She closed the book and said, "Look at you, you left a sweat stain on my couch."

"Sorry, Ma, it's like an oven in here."

"You'd sweat less if you lost some weight."

"Jesus, Ma." He wiped his hand over his head again and said, "Look, I got to get going. I'll see you next week."

BARB HAD BARELY NOTICED the cars when she first moved into the trailer park. She was busy with other things — still in the middle of her divorce and working full-time at city hall, where she made sure the bylaw complaints were all filed correctly and followed up on. Her living room window faced the intersection at the entrance to the trailer park; anyone coming in came to a stop with their lights shining into her home, through her blinds and reflecting off the TV. It was a minor annoyance, but one she thought was temporary.

She hadn't wanted to move to the trailer park and didn't intend to stay; it was, after all, a trailer park. But she didn't have much of a choice. Two months after Mark moved to the city for college, her ex left her for that whore of a waitress from the scuzzy diner out on the highway. Their house was put up for sale, her ex moved in with the waitress, and she was forced out on the street by a strongly worded legal note. There weren't many options in town — rentals were either horrible apartment blocks full of divorced construction workers and drunks, or straight-up crack dens.

Her real estate agent sold her on the idea of buying a trailer: she had just enough money of her own for the down payment, it would hold its value, and it would be easy enough to get out of when the divorce was finalized and her half of the house money arrived. Barb could even hold on to it and rent it out after she got a new place; it was a good investment. And it was a nice trailer park, the agent had said. Originally a campground, it was situated at the base of a mountain on one side, with a river on the other. The nearby highway was blocked by a noise-cancelling wall, and the industrial park next door contained *light* industry, not very loud at all. And you couldn't beat the location, a ten-minute walk to town or a two-minute drive.

Barb should have known the real estate agent was a liar. She found out later it was the same woman who was helping her ex buy a new place; they probably shared a good laugh about sticking Barb in a trailer park.

It was a horrible place. The walk to town was impossible. There were no sidewalks and the trucks speeding in and out of the industrial park at all hours had no regard for pedestrians. The highway was loud and the mountain was nothing more than a hill where local kids hung out to do drugs and have sex. The river was just a bit upstream from the treatment plant, and any time there was flooding, it would back up and the whole park would smell of the city's business. And the trailer park was anything but quiet—there were naked children running around, kids drinking and doing drugs, and adults doing the same. And there were dealers too.

Barb went to work, kept to herself, and let her neighbours know she wasn't at their level; she spoke to no one and actively discouraged anyone from speaking to her. It was, she'd kept telling herself, temporary.

MARK BANGED INTO THE screen door with the groceries. It bounced off the wall and back into him. So loud, Barb thought, so sloppy.

"Hi, Ma." He dropped the bags onto the table and started to load the microwaveable meals into the freezer. He struggled to make room, tilting and forcing, eventually pulling everything out and starting over. A car entered the trailer park; she had to squint to get the licence plate. She wrote it down.

"What is that?" She couldn't believe her son could move so quick. He was standing over her, looking at her ledger.

"It's my book," she said, pulling her forearm over it. He leaned over further to look. A drop of sweat landed on her forearm.

"Oh, sorry Ma."

"That's disgusting."

"Ma, I sweat. I don't know what you want me to do about it."

"Lose weight. Fat traps heat."

"Anyways, what's that book? Is it all licence plate numbers?"

"It is."

"Why?"

"We have trouble with drug dealers. If someone looks suspicious, I write down their licence number."

"And the time?"

She covered the book more. "Yes, of course."

"Why?"

"Someone has to do it. Kids are so bad these days. With the drugs."

"Uh-huh."

She slammed the book shut when he stooped down to look closer.

"Ma, why would you write down my licence plate? You think I'm selling drugs?"

"Of course not. I didn't know it was you until you pulled into my driveway."

He looked at her with that weak, soft face. She could never understand where he picked that up from — uncertainty, an inability to be direct. She wasn't like that. His father wasn't either. He would lie, hide, and cheat, but he was direct when he needed to be.

He said, "I mean, that's a bit strange, isn't it?"

"No."

He sat on the couch and looked like he was thinking; she could practically hear the gears moving inside his head. Before he could come up with something to say, Barb said, "Get off the couch! It took me an hour to clean your sweat stains last week."

"Jesus, Ma." He got up and they both looked at the couch. There was a wet mark where his back had been. He ran his hand over his hairless dome and said, "Look, I got to go."

BARB WAS AWARDED ALIMONY in the divorce but never saw a dime. And she didn't get any money from the sale of the house either. According to her ex's lawyer, the house sold under-value and much of that money was used to pay off debts and bad investments she hadn't known about.

She knew something was up. Her lawyer was a useless twit who'd been friends with her ex, and he obviously hadn't been looking out for her best interests. She got a new lawyer, who, after she paid him for six months of work, let her know that her ex, technically, had no money; it had all been transferred into his new wife's name. Barb would not be able to get her hands on it.

Barb didn't accept that. She was sure a judge would see things her way, if only she could prove there was money. She started driving by her ex's new house after work. She bought a disposable camera and took photos of renovations. She saw his car was gone for two weeks — probably a vacation, which she confirmed with his employer when she called pretending to be a customer. She started keeping notes for the judge.

One day, after looking at his house for a long time to be certain no one was home, she walked around back to the shed. She took a full garbage bag and headed home. Going through the old coffee grounds and apple cores, she found six receipts, but none for anything flashy or suspicious. Still, it was enough to keep her going back for more. She would take days off to be sure both her ex and the whore were at work, and then she'd sneak around back and grab a bag, replacing it with the last one she stole. Eventually, she found enough receipts for big purchases to prove that he was hiding money. If he could afford a ride-on lawnmower and a new stereo for his car, he could pay her alimony.

And then a bailiff came to her door and served her a restraining order. When she realized what was happening, she became frantic. No, she said, it was all wrong. She was doing these things to prove that her ex-husband was the criminal, not her. By then, neighbours were looking out their doors at her. She saw herself, yelling at a police officer, in a trailer park, in her nightgown. She slammed the door in the bailiff's face.

For three months she argued her case everywhere she could. She took it to the police, the courts. She refused to get a lawyer—they'd only ever ripped her off—so it took her a long time to bully her way into a hearing. In the meantime, she let everyone know what a scumbag her ex had been: cheating, stealing, refusing to pay what he owed her.

Mark eventually got involved. He came down from college and had the nerve to tell her she was becoming obsessive and should just let it go. He didn't understand what she'd gone through—to have to live in a trailer park, hand-to-mouth, after she'd slaved away to raise Mark and keep his father happy.

Mark told her that he was trying, really trying, but it was hard. He said his dad wasn't as bad as she thought, that if she could see his side, maybe they could leave all the unpleasantness behind them. Barb asked what other side was there? His dad was a cheating so-and-so. But it was so like Mark to side with his father, since he was paying for Mark's school with that whore's money. Mark left after that.

A month later, a judge upheld the restraining order. Garbage, he explained, was not admissible evidence.

• • •

"I'VE BEEN THINKING ABOUT your little project," Mark said as he put away the groceries. He opened the peanut butter and peeled the protective cover off, dropping it in the garbage. As though she couldn't do it herself; her arthritis wasn't that bad.

Barb asked, "What project?"

"The cars. The licence plates."

She watched him struggle to reach the cupboard. His belly mashed up against the counter, divided by it. How had she raised a son who cared so little for his appearance?

"If you're worried about security, we could get you a camera to put in the window. I can hook it up to your computer."

"I don't like computers. I barely use the one you bought me. A waste of money, that."

Mark ran his hand over his head and sighed. "Well, you don't need to like it. I can set it up so that you don't have to do anything. It will just record, and if anything happens, I can come over and go through the tape to look at the cars. You won't need to do a thing."

"I wouldn't want the expense."

"A webcam is, like, twenty dollars."

"You don't need to waste money on that. Why not spend it on a gym membership?"

"Ma! Jesus."

"Well, you just spend so much time on computers. I think some exercise would be good for you."

"Ma, come on."

"I'm just saying you should worry more about your own business than mine."

"I know, Ma. But I think this will be good for you."

"You're telling me what would be good for me?"

Mark sighed and slumped, like jelly freed from its mould.

Barb shuddered.

Her son said, "Look, I got to run."

BARB HADN'T SEEN MUCH of Mark after they'd fought over the divorce and her attempts to prove his dad was a scumbag. He came by on holidays, but never seemed to want to be there. Eventually he just starting calling instead. He had always favoured his father; she didn't need him in her life.

Barb spent a few years trying to get enough money together to move out of the trailer park, but ran up against endless setbacks. Her car was stolen, probably by one of the druggies in the park. Then the park flooded and she had to re-floor her trailer, only to find out her insurance wouldn't cover it *after* the work was done — they considered flooding a known risk of living there. And she was forced to pay a large fine or serve jail time after her ex reported her for violating the restraining order, even though she had a perfectly good reason for being in his subdivision. The judge did not believe that she was visiting her Avon lady. "Don't they come to you?" he'd asked.

Eventually, she settled into a routine. She woke up in the morning, went to the coffee shop downtown, and then to work. She stayed late, ate at the Denny's on the highway, and got home in time to watch an hour of TV before falling asleep.

But then she got laid off. She was given a small severance, enough to carry her to when her retirement would start coming in if she lived cheaply. There wasn't money for much, so she started spending her days inside. TV was cheap; she watched a lot of it but found daytime TV distasteful — people airing their problems on national TV, reminding her of her neighbours. She spent her days rolling her eyes in disgust and flipping over to the news, only to flip back to see what new low these shows could deliver.

A couple of months into her forced retirement she heard a car idling outside her window. She leaned over the back of her couch and looked through the curtains, then got on with her day without a second thought. A few days later, she heard an idling car again. It looked like the same car, and it was around the same time of day, she thought. A few days later, there it was again. This time she knew for sure it was the same one, and the same time. She was ready for it the next day.

She watched it pull into the trailer park through a crack in her curtains. She instinctively ducked when it came to a stop at the intersection, then felt silly and looked up. The Anderson boy from trailer 34 was handing a bag through the window. She couldn't tell, but it looked like he got something small back. Then the two did some sort of slap, high-five handshake thing. The Anderson boy left, and the car turned around in the intersection, hopping up on Barb's lawn. At the very last minute, Barb thought she should get the licence plate. Between the car pulling away and her finding a pen and an envelope to write on, she only managed to get three letters: AFG. She wasn't sure what to do with that information, but thought it might be important.

The car came back the next day. She marked down the time and got the full licence plate. It happened every Monday to Friday. She started keeping half an eye on the window while she went about her business, watching for the drop, hoping to see proof of her suspicions that it was drugs.

She started noticing other things though. One day, a car entered the park and stopped a long time at the sign before it turned in and drove slowly out of sight. Under a minute later, it appeared again from the other direction, turned slowly, and left the park. She wrote the plate number down just to be safe; that was certainly a suspicious way to drive.

Soon, Barb bought a notebook and drew columns for plate numbers, arrival times, departure times, and notes, where she wrote things like "Drove slowly, looking," or "mailman," or "Indians." She left the notebook open on the back of the couch while she craned around to look through the window.

A month in, she started to get a serious ache in her arm and back from all the twisting. It was then that Barb rearranged the house. She moved the couch to the opposite wall. She got a small writing desk from her bedroom and placed it under the window, with a kitchen chair beside it. Then she set up the TV where she could see it while sitting at the desk.

She filled up the first notebook in two months.

"IT'LL FREE UP YOUR days." Her son had wedged his body in between the desk and the wall, groping for the sockets while staring at nothing. "You can get out of the house. Walking will be good for your back."

"You're a doctor now? I can barely get across the room."

Barb was livid. He'd come in, dropped off the groceries, and gone right for her desk. She had told him not to mess with anything but he'd just done it. His stupid fat body looked like a lump of dough slopping down the wall. She stood above it, wishing she were big enough to haul him out like when he was a toddler.

"Ma, you got to go out every now and then. It's better for you than sitting around."

"And you, when do you go out? When do you get exercise? What do you know about it?"

His head slumped to the desk, but then he pulled himself up. He sat down in the chair. Barb wasn't sure it would survive his bulk. He started opening windows on her computer.

Barb said, "Don't mess with that. I need to be able to find my programs."

"I'm just going to set up the webcam."

"Last time you were on it, everything disappeared."

"Ma, the computer updated. The folder icons just changed. Everything was where it was."

"Well, I couldn't find them. What's that, what are you doing?"

"Just downloading a program, don't worry."

"Am I going to get hijacked? I get warnings."

"You're not going to get hijacked."

"How do you know? I hear all the time about them tying up your computer, holding it hostage."

"Ma, if 'they' hold all your 1950s murder mystery programs hostage, I'll come over and replace them."

"How can you talk to me like that, I'm your mother."

"I know, Ma."

Things popped up and disappeared all over her screen. She was surprised at how quickly her son's fat fingers could type; it was like watching sausage links flap in the wind. No wonder he couldn't keep a girl. She briefly thought of his father's meaty mitts pawing at her.

"What's that? Who can see that?"

It was her, on the screen. The computer-her lagged a half-second behind real-life-her. She scowled. Computer-her scowled back.

"Only you can see it."

"Because I hear about them hijacking webcams and watching."

"Well, once again, 'they' probably won't bother. And besides, the camera will be pointing outside." He put the webcam on her station by the window and pointed it outside. Then he pulled the curtains so that just a crack was open. The intersection appeared on her screen.

"Now you won't have people looking in either."

She sat down, then stood back up. She said, "But this is running all the time?"

"Yeah."

"Won't it cost money? The electricity?"

"Ma, I don't think you even know how to turn off your computer. It's not going to cost anything extra."

"Sarcasm is an awful trait."

He sighed, but went on. "It's motion-activated, so it will come on when a car goes by. Watch."

He clicked a few things and the screen went blank. They sat quietly. Neither said anything for a few minutes. Then Mark said, "Well, I guess there's not a lot of tra—"

A car appeared on the screen. It was from the neighbourhood. After it rounded the corner, the screen went blank again.

"So?" Barb asked.

"It's saved. Now let's say that guy goes and sells everyone a bunch of those nasty drugs, I come over and…" He slapped the keyboard for a minute, and then the footage appeared again. He made it stop and somehow zoomed in. "There you go: FHY 863. You've solved the crime. And you don't have to sit here all day."

"I don't know…"

"Ma, it'll change your life."

• • •

BARB HAD CALLED THE police once, three years before. She'd never gotten to the bottom of the Anderson boy's drop-offs; they'd continued for six months, then stopped out of the blue. But the boy grew, and after a few years, started getting into serious trouble. He seemed to have his run of the place; his mother, who was just as bad as him, was never around. She'd hooked up with some biker, Barb heard. The boy never seemed to go to school. He came home at all hours, and people were coming to visit him all the time. Young girls wearing tank tops that showed everyone everything. The useless boys, now pretty much men, leering at the girls, all of them drinking and getting into trouble. For three weekends in a row there were parties loud enough to hear in her trailer. Her noise complaints got her nowhere and the ruckus kept her up all night while she marked down all the licence plates of the cars coming and going and thought of all the horrible things she would have done to the kids.

The morning after the fourth weekend party, she called the police again and insisted they send someone. She had, she said, several crimes to report—and no, she didn't want to file a report over the phone with a receptionist, she wanted to talk to a real police officer. Three hours later a police cruiser pulled up to her trailer.

Barb was ready, waiting on her steps. Before the two officers got out of the car she told them about the drug deals, the noise, the parties. The young people, the sex, the drinking. She said she had proof and brought them inside where she showed them the book. She explained about the cars coming and going, the drug dealing. She told them about the noise and how it was the Anderson boy and all the trouble he brought with him. The officers had started to write down what she said, but by the time she was done, they had both closed their notebooks.

The two officers looked at each other before the older one responded. "You write down every car's licence plate?"

"Not every one. Just the suspicious people."

He flipped through her book. She reached out and grabbed it. The officers exchanged a look.

"They're bringing drugs in here."

"This isn't proof, ma'am; it's just a bunch of licence plate numbers."

"But I see them."

"Look, we can't do much with this. But we can go talk to the kid—Anderson, was it?—about the noise. And we can keep an eye on things."

They left her after she explained to them they were doing things the wrong way. The cruiser drove around the corner toward the Anderson's trailer. Barb went back inside to her station by the window. A few minutes later, the police drove out. One of the officers flashed her a thumbs-up before they turned.

A few minutes after that, the Anderson boy's car pulled up to the intersection. He rolled down the window and held up his middle finger. She stepped away from the window.

SHE SAW HER SON pull up to the trailer. He didn't take anything out of the car, but did walk across the lawn to straighten the rocks that formed the border of her garden. He waved at her and smiled his stupid, slack grin.

He came in without knocking and said, "Hey Ma, I thought you might like to come grocery shopping with me today. It would be good for you to…Ma, where's your computer?"

"I packed it up. It's more trouble than it's worth."

Mark let his arms flap down. They didn't hang straight; they couldn't with his gut sticking out the sides the way it did. He said, "Ma, I'm trying to help you. You need to get out of the house more."

"You're one to talk. You should get out of the house more. Look at you. How did I end up with a son who could let himself go like that?"

"Ma. Just shut up a minute."

"How dare you!"

He ran his hand over his forehead. "Ma, I'm really trying here. You got back in touch with me; we're seeing each other again. I want to help, but you're being real awful. I mean, you're becoming a shut-in."

"Better a shut-in than a fat slob."

"Jesus, Ma. Look, I know I'm carrying a few extra pounds. But that's not what we're talking about. You're just going to sit here and stare out the window recording licence plates so you can report crimes that don't happen? What's the point in that? I want to help you, Ma."

She was surprised that he was shouting; he never shouted. She wasn't sure what to do, so she let her head fall down and she began to cry. Quiet dignified sniffles into a tissue she plucked from a box on her desk. Her son didn't move.

Barb bent down again and sobbed harder. When she didn't hear him moving, she said, "It's just…it's been so hard for me, you know?"

Mark said, "You know, Ma. Dad said you'd do this."

She stopped crying and looked up. "Don't you bring your father into this."

"He knows you. He said you'd fight and bully, and if that didn't work you'd cry. Just like when I was a kid. Just like when you were married."

"How could you listen to that lying, cheating—"

"You know what, Ma? I'm done with this. I thought we could see each other, have a relationship again. But you have never once been anything like nice to me. It's not worth it for me. I've got to go."

"But my back..."

"If you packed up the computer and threw it out, you'll be fine to pick up groceries. Bye, Ma."

Barb sat on the couch and watched Mark's car leave.

Her son, she'd always known, was ungrateful. Always had been. And she didn't need him coming around anyways. His girth making her home look small, heating up the room with rancid body smells barely masked by his terrible deodorant. Just like his father. And why bring *him* into it? What did Mark know about his father? But he'd side with his dad, of course; he was his father's son. If she hadn't carried him nine months, she'd have been sure he wasn't hers. He certainly didn't get much from her.

Barb's train of thought was broken by a car pulling into the trailer park.

Little to Lose

When the bill came, Debbie was relieved to see the waitress had included the seniors' discount without prompting. She went over to the ATM and punched in sixty dollars and got an insufficient funds message. She tried forty. Two bills shuffled out at her. The slip let her know she was just eight dollars away from the limit of her overdraft.

Back at the table she made a show of carefully looking over the bill and then her money while the waitress waited. Debbie said, "Oh, I'm sorry. I didn't take out enough money. I need to hold on to *this* cash"—she held up the two twenties—"but I could use some change." She bit her lip like she was puzzling out a problem. "So, can I put eight on my debit, then have you break this twenty for the rest? Is that okay?"

The waitress didn't care.

Debbie left the restaurant and walked across the parking lot. She had thirty-eight dollars in cash and her overdraft was at its limit. Her Visa was at ten thousand, with a minimum payment due the next week. Her other credit cards were maxed out at five and six thousand dollars, but their payments weren't due for three weeks, so she didn't have to worry about them. Her paycheque was coming in later that week, but it would only just cover rent and not any of the bills, which were so far behind she couldn't even think about them—which reminded her that she did have to worry about the car insurance, even though there was really nothing to do about it and she'd been driving uninsured for a month anyways. The main thing was the minimum payment on her main credit card: fifty dollars. An amount she was twelve dollars short of.

The thirty-eight dollars cash she had was as good as useless since it wasn't enough to actually cover any of the bills, so she thought she might as well try to make something of it. By then she had walked across the parking lot and crossed the street to where the town's tiny casino was housed.

She walked through the sliding doors onto the thick electric-patterned carpet. She tried to slip by the security guard while he chatted with two regulars, but he caught her eye and smiled. "Hold on there,

LITTLE TO LOSE   75

miss," he said. "You look too young to be coming in here." She made as if to pull her wallet out of her purse and the guard just laughed and waved her by, saying, "Nice to see you again, Debbie. Good luck."

She went straight to the bank of quarter slots near the back wall, ignoring the five-dollar machines by the door. The payouts on those were big, but the money disappeared too quick; if she could play longer, she had a better chance of winning, Debbie figured. Six machines grouped together were tied in with a TV show she liked. She fed a twenty into one and her credits appeared at the bottom of the screen. She pressed the Bet Max button.

Shapes on the screen spun while the theme from the TV show played quietly in the background, blending in with the noise of all the other machines. The shapes settled into five columns and rows, and red lines appeared connecting the patterns that matched. Her credits went up. She played on, sometimes three or four lines connected, sometimes none. When half her money was gone, Debbie switched to the next machine over and started betting less. Less risk meant less payout, but she could play longer. She kept at it and then everything lit up and the machine said, "Bazinga!" Everything connected, but she had only bet on two lines. Her credits went up, but not as much as they could have. She was angry at herself for the missed opportunity. She started betting more and her credits went steadily down to zero.

Debbie went to a different game and fed in the last of her money, telling herself she'd cash out with ten dollars left. But when she got down to that amount she decided ten wasn't enough to really do anything with anyways, so she might as well keep going. A small win took her back up to twenty, which wasn't much better than ten, so she kept going and then her money was all gone.

The security guard was different when she left; he didn't look at her. The parking lot was dark. Debbie walked to the restaurant and got into her car. The engine turned, coughed, caught. It only took her five minutes to get to her building; there was no traffic this time of night.

The elevator took a long time to get to her floor, with its buzzing fluorescent light. She passed no one in the hall, then got into her apartment, tossed her jacket and purse on the couch, and lay down on top of them.

DEBBIE'S PHONE BUZZED HER awake. She dug it out of her coat pocket and tried to turn off what she thought was the alarm but instead picked up a call. It took her a second to register her brother's voice asking if anyone was there. She brought the phone to her face and said yes. They made plans to have coffee that afternoon.

She scraped all the old food off plates into the garbage and stashed them in the dishwasher. She swept and decided it would be better to shower than to tidy more. When she came out there was no time for curlers so she wrapped her hair in a scarf and then the buzzer sounded. She hit the button to unlock the front door and took a quick look around. She tossed a newspaper over a pile of unopened mail just as Dan let himself in. They hugged and talked about how it had been too long. Debbie made a pot of coffee while Dan sat at the kitchen table and set up the crib board.

Dan skunked her in the first two games, counting out his winning hands without much enthusiasm. While he shuffled, he told Debbie that his kids were starting college in the city and both had found places to live and that his daughter had moved in with her boyfriend. He talked about his lighting store and the economy and how it looked like it was going to be a rough year, but it could never be as bad as it was back in ninety-six. Then he asked Debbie about her grandkids and job. The kids were good, she said, even though she didn't see much of them. The job was still just part-time.

Dan started a new game and they both looked over their cards and told each other what garbage they had.

Debbie said, "Fifteen two, fifteen four, and there is no more." She moved her peg.

Dan said, "I hear you've been over at the new casino."

Debbie looked up. "I went over once to see what it looked like."

Dan put his cards down and moved his peg. He said, "Debbie. I hear it's more than once. And from a few people." Debbie didn't say anything. "You know, there's nothing wrong with gambling. I like Vegas as much as anyone, but that's different—there you can take in a show, there's entertainment. That place is just slots and Keno. You can't win, and there's no fun to distract you when you're losing."

Debbie shuffled the cards and dealt another hand. Dan left his cards lying face down while Debbie sorted hers. Dan said, "I know things have been tight."

"I'm doing okay."

They played quietly after that. Dan won another game. He asked if they should play another round. Debbie said she actually had plans and needed to get ready. At the door, Dan pulled Debbie into a hug. He lingered by the open door and said, "I know it's been a hard few years for you. You know you don't need to worry about the money you owe me."

Debbie thanked him and closed the door. She put their cups in the sink and walked out onto the balcony and watched the cars driving by below.

• • •

NEAR THE END OF the month, Debbie gave in and checked her bank account online. Her work cheque had cleared and there was just enough to cover rent, but they were threatening to cut off the power so she had to deal with that first. She called her bank and let them know about her long history with them and explained that she had to make some unexpected loans to family members and wondered if they could extend her overdraft. The voice on the phone let her know that he was very sorry to say he could not.

She tried one of her credit card companies. They *could* give her a higher limit, but that would change her interest rate to something less favourable. She okayed it, then paid off her hydro bill. She put a little on her phone to keep them happy, and paid the minimum on one of her other credit cards. Then she headed out for lunch. After, she explained to the waitress that she forgot her debit card at home and wondered if she could do cash back on the credit card. The waitress said she could.

Debbie wanted to make her twenty last, so she stuck to the penny slots where she couldn't bet more than ten cents at a time. She didn't like these games. The screens had ten rows and dozens of shapes; there were more ways to win and more to lose, but it was just a swirling mess of lights that was impossible for her to follow. Sometimes her credits went up, sometimes down. She was never too sure why.

"Deb?"

Debbie turned around. Valerie Marston squealed and threw her arms around Debbie. They tried to remember the last time they'd seen each other and figured it must have been when their boys graduated back in ninety-nine. Could they believe it was that long? "And imagine, meeting at this shithole!" Val grabbed Debbie's forearm and laughed.

Debbie said, "I was just over at the mall. I've been wondering what this place looked like inside since it opened."

"Oh, shit. I come here every couple weeks for the Keno. Rick hates it. I blow half my pay sometimes." Val laughed again. "But what the hell, right? You only live once."

Debbie said she probably should be going and hit the button to cash out. They left together and at Val's car they hugged and made plans to see each other again. Once Val was clear of the parking lot, Debbie turned around and went back into the casino.

DEBBIE'S SON VISITED WITH the grandkids for her birthday. He brought a small cake and a present that turned out to be a new coffee mug with a picture of her grandkids on it. Debbie divided the cake and when it was gone the two boys started tearing around the apartment. One of the boys knocked a stack of mail off a chair, so Braden finally turned on the TV and sat them down in front of it. He carried the envelopes back to the kitchen table and handed them to his mom. "Not opening your mail?"

"Oh, it's just junk."

"You doing okay, Mom?"

"I'm doing okay."

"I was at Uncle Dan's."

"Dan doesn't know what he's talking about."

"He can help, Mom."

Debbie got up and poured herself a glass of water, then went into the living room where the kids were watching TV. She tickled her grandson and sat down beside him. Braden joined her and they watched cartoons for bit and then Debbie said she had some plans that afternoon and they needed to clear out soon. The boys ran around getting their stuff together and then they were all at the door trying to leave.

She gave them a few minutes to get to the car before she pulled on her jacket and headed out. There was a fifty in one of the pockets. She was sure it hadn't been there before and then she thought: Braden. She decided to leave it on the table and return it later, but then she was in the elevator, slowly heading down to the lobby with the fifty still in her hand.

At the bank machine, she saw that a work cheque

had cleared, which put her account just under zero. With the overdraft, that gave her a couple hundred to work with. She paid the minimum on two of her credit cards and fifty on her phone bill because they called every day to tell her they were going to cut her off. That maxed out her overdraft, and hydro was due and she was still driving without insurance and rent was coming up again. But she had that fifty, which wasn't enough for rent or the months of insurance she owed anyways, and it was found money besides.

She tried a different approach with the machines. Rather than abandoning one that wasn't paying out, she stayed with it — the more the losses added up, the better her chances of a win, she figured. She fed the fifty-dollar bill into a machine and went down to twenty before hitting a jackpot that sent her to a hundred. She switched machines, again, waiting for a big payout. She lost steadily, with enough occasional small wins to keep her going. When she levelled out at fifty she thought about cashing out and putting the money aside for Braden, but she was sure that she would get another win because there was no way a machine could lose that much. Her credits went down and she started betting two or three credits rather than the max. Her credits dwindled. With less than ten dollars left she decided to bet it all at once and be done with it.

A light started flashing and she thought she'd somehow set off an alarm before she realized all the lines were connected.

A FEW WEEKS LATER, Debbie got pulled over coming home from work. She asked the officer what seemed to be the problem and he told her that her licence plate sticker showed that her insurance had expired. She let the officer know she was sure that couldn't be right. She dug out her papers and told him how shocked she was and that she felt so silly that it had slipped her mind and promised she'd go in and renew her insurance right away. The officer asked her if she wouldn't mind holding on for just one second and took her licence back to his cruiser. He came back less friendly; it seemed she'd already been given two warnings about the expired insurance.

She waited with the officer for the tow truck to take her car away, then started walking home along the highway. It was going to cost two hundred and fifty to get the car out of impound and the cop had given her fines beside. The fines could wait but if she didn't get her car back right away she'd be charged another twenty-five a day. She knew her overdraft was at its limit and most of her pay had to go to rent at the end of the week, but she figured there was at least eighty dollars extra. But that wasn't the two-fifty she needed today, let alone the three-seventy-five it would be by the time she had any money at all. And then there was paying off the insurance on top of all that.

Debbie unlocked the front door of her building and got in the elevator. The doors closed on the fake lobby plants. A minute later, the doors slid open to reveal the fake plants on her floor. She walked by them to her apartment.

She took the pile of unopened mail to the kitchen table and fished out her bank statement. It was three months old and she knew how much was in there anyways. She looked in her purse and didn't see much, then flipped it upside down to let everything fall out. There was about four bucks in loose change. She checked her other purses, then her coat pockets, her jeans, some drawers, and between the couch cushions. She slumped against the edge of the couch and wondered what her TV was worth; it was an old one, not even a flat screen. Probably wouldn't even get picked up off the curb.

Finally, she called Dan and said, "You won't believe what happened…"

THEY MET AT THE impound lot and Dan paid everything off without saying much to Debbie. He followed her back to her apartment in his car and parked beside her in the lot. Debbie asked if he needed something. Dan said he was coming up so they could sort this out. Debbie tried to say it was fine, but Dan just followed her in.

"You don't need to worry about me."

"Do you think I believe you got towed for accidentally parking in a handicap spot?"

"What do you—"

"Your insurance is two months' expired, Debbie. You don't have the cash to renew it, or to get your car out of impound. You're not even making eye contact with me right now."

Debbie looked him right in the eyes. "I'm fine."

"No, you're not." Dan sighed and sat down at the kitchen table. He said, "You're broke, but you shouldn't be."

Debbie left him sitting there. She went into the bathroom and ran the taps while she thought of how to get rid of her brother. When she came out, he was by the door, going through her mail.

"That's illegal."

"Then call the cops. Come on. Look at this." He held up the envelopes. "Past due. Last notice. You don't even open it."

"So, I'm a bit behind."

"Debbie, it's more than a bit. I can help."

She thought about kicking him out. But then, she was broke. Even if she didn't pay Dan back for getting her car out of the impound, her entire next paycheque was going to rent, which meant she was going to miss her credit card minimums. Which meant the debt was going to climb.

Debbie went into the kitchen and sat down. Dan followed her in with the mail. He said, "Let's go over this."

He had her find her insurance papers, tickets, rent receipts, anything that could help sort out where the money had gone. They laid the papers out on the kitchen table and Dan opened the mail and divided everything up — anything from her bank went in one pile, credit card companies in another, hydro bills, insurance. When he was done, the table was completely covered with stacks of paper.

Then he sorted each pile, finding the most recent bills and scrapping the old. He started jotting down numbers, adding things up and making notes. Debbie tried to explain where the money was — one thing to pay off another to pay off another — but Dan told her that the reasons didn't change anything: they were debts that needed to be paid. He said, "You'll have to live cheaper. Get rid of cable, get rid of the car."

"I need the car."

"It will take you half an hour to walk to work. You can do that."

"But what will people say?"

"That you like to walk."

"They'll think I can't afford a car."

"You *can't* afford a car."

Another half-hour later Dan had laid it all out. The piles of paper, the years of debt, put into clean columns, various interest rates calculated, debts divided into the have-to-pays, the would-be-nice-to-pays, the can-waits. "You've been chasing the small debts and not worrying about the big picture. You'll have to call some of these companies, tell them that they'll get their money, but after the deadlines. They'll go for it. It's better for them to get money out of you late than not at all."

Debbie looked hopelessly at the numbers. It was worse than she'd thought. Dan continued, "There's a lot of debt, but you make enough money to live and should be able to manage. It's bad, but it's not impossible. You have a job, you have your health. There are lots of people worse off than you. But you have to stop gambling."

"I barely—"

"Debbie."

"It's not like it's all losses. I won two thousand dollars last month."

"Where's that?"

"I paid off some things."

"Those things needed to be paid off because of the gambling. Come on, Deb. You're smarter than that."

They sat there a while, Dan repeated a few points, went over who needed to be called, saying that he was sure he could get his accountant to make calls if anyone gave her trouble. The main thing, he kept saying, was to make her payments and work away at the principal.

They went through everything once more, then Dan suggested they go for dinner. Debbie said no, she really needed to be alone and think this through. Dan took forty dollars out of his wallet and put it on the table. "Take it. You'll need groceries."

At the door, they hugged. Dan said, "You can do this. I promise."

DEBBIE SAT DOWN AT the table and looked over the notes. The debts, added into one number, broken down into payments to be made in the years ahead. Her future, laid out in interest rates and pay schedules. Money not yet earned but already spoken for. If her only expense was the debt, it would take three years to pay off. But with rent, food, and living her life, at her current wage . . . Maybe she could get a better-paying job. Maybe that would shave a few months off, maybe a year. But that was so little, and the debt so much.

But there was that forty dollars, not factored into the numbers. She pulled on her shoes and coat. It was so little to lose, after all; forty dollars was worth even the small chance of something better.

Harold

Harold bounced his van up onto the curb and tapped the horn twice. Maggie, across the street at the bus stop, shook her head. He rolled down the window and waved her over. She shook her head again and pointed up the street. Harold shouted, "Come on, I'm heading your way."

She ran across the street and said, "If my dad sees you picking me up, he'll kill me."

"I was driving by and thought you'd want a ride. Sorry."

She went around the front of the van and climbed in. "Just go."

Harold shifted the van into gear and then put his hand on her thigh, just under the hem of her kilt. Maggie shifted toward the door and pulled down the sun flap. She looked at herself in the mirror and put on a new layer of lip gloss and added some more eye shadow to her already black eyelids. Harold told her she looked great and reached around the back of her neck to give it a rub. Her shoulders hunched. He said, "So what happened to you last night?"

"My grandma was over for dinner and my dad's really cracked down on me being on the phone after eight." She undid the top two buttons of her shirt.

Harold leaned back to get a better angle and said, "I was kind of hoping you'd come over tonight. You could tell your folks you're staying at Allison's again."

"I actually have plans. A friend's party."

"Oh cool, I can drive us there?"

"I don't know, it's sort of just kids from school."

"Give me a call before to let me know?"

"I'll be over at Allison's. But I'll try."

She told him to drop her off a couple blocks away from the school so her teachers wouldn't see her getting out of his van. He leaned over for a kiss that landed on her cheek and tried to get his hand back on her thigh. She slipped out the door and said, "I got to get to class."

HAROLD'S MOM BANGED HER foot on the floor above him and shouted, "Har-reee. Phone! Har-reee. Phone!"

He picked up and shouted at the ceiling, "I got it, Mom."

"Har-reee. Phone." She banged the floor again.

"Mom! I got it."

He spoke into the phone. "Maggie?"

She said, "It's so weird you have a landline."

And from upstairs, "Har-reee," with more banging.

"I've got it!"

Then his mom's voice, on the phone now, asked, "Har-reee. You there?"

He said into the phone, "Yes, Mom, thank you."

"You need to cut the lawn."

"I will, Mom, tomorrow. Bye."

"Bye Har-reee."

"Hello?"

Maggie said, "Allison's sister got called in to work. Would you mind booting for us?"

"Well, I sort of made other plans when I found out you weren't free."

"Oh, that's fine, we can ask someone in front of the liquor store."

"No, no, that's okay. I'll come down."

Harold drove down to the coffee shop. Maggie, Allison, and a few of the guys from their class were sitting around the patio. Harold got out of his van and Allison said, "Hi, Har-reee!"

"Yeah, hi."

"You get that lawn mowed?"

Maggie hit Allison's shoulder and told her to shut up and Allison laughed.

There was nowhere for Harold to sit. He grabbed a chair from inside and hovered with it, waiting for Allison to shift over and make room for him. Matt, one of the guy friends, asked everyone to move down for Harold. He dropped his chair in and said, "Thanks."

Then the guys were talking about a show their band had booked at the community centre and how they had a lead on a place they could play in the city.

Harold said, "Yeah, well my band is thinking about going on tour again pretty quick. You can only play the George and Dragon so many times, you know?"

Allison asked, "Where was that last tour to again, Harry?"

"We went down the coast to Oregon."

Matt said, "Cool, man."

And Allison said, "Yeah, cool. When was that again?"

Before Harold could answer, Maggie said, "Why don't we go get the drinks."

Maggie and Allison each gave Harold a ten for some cider and the guys pooled together to come up with enough for a case and a mickey of whisky. Harold got up. When no one else did, he said to Maggie, "You coming?"

Allison said, "We're still waiting for a couple of people, so we got to stay here."

Harold tried to be cool but made it clear he wasn't going to run their errand alone. Matt volunteered to go along. There was really no way for Harold to say no.

They drove the three blocks to the liquor store. Harold turned up the stereo and Matt asked him what they were listening to. Harold told him and he said, "Cool, old school." And then said it sounded like some band Harold had never heard of.

"More like those guys sound like *this*."

Back at the coffee shop, Harold asked them what the deal was with the party. Matt said, "Oh, it's just this kid whose folks are out of town."

And Allison said, "But it's going to be small, just friends. The neighbours ratted on him last time."

"But you should totally come along," Matt said.

And Allison said, "Isn't it weird for you to go to a high-school party?"

Maggie kept quiet and Harold eventually said, "Well, there's a show I might check out later tonight anyways."

One of the other guys started talking about a show in the city he'd gotten a fake ID for. Matt snuck some whisky into his coffee and everyone started talking about bands Harold didn't know. Harold tried to get

Maggie's attention but she kept looking intently at whoever was talking. After a while, Matt said they should all go to the park and have a few pre-party drinks there. Harold jumped in and said, "There's always cops checking the park, we should go for a drive around the lake."

Allison wasn't into that, but Matt and the other guys were, so they all ended up in the van, heading out of town on the logging road that led to the far end of the lake. Harold drove them to one of the little beaches and parked.

By the time Harold got a beer from the back of his van, all the guys were sitting on a log near the beach and Maggie and Allison were on a boulder beside them. The only spot left was right on the end of the log. Harold sat and held his hand out to Maggie, then let it drop.

Someone brought out some weed and passed it around; Matt took a swig of the whisky. Maggie and Allison passed their cider back and forth. Harold got up and stood behind Maggie. He put his hands on her shoulders. She looked up at him and smiled. He bent down and kissed the top of her head. Allison said, "Come pee with me," and she and Maggie went off to the woods.

Harold sat on their rock and Matt came over and sat beside him. He took another sip of whisky. Harold said, "Watch it with that."

Matt said, "It's cool, man. I heard Keith Jones from the Who used to drink three bottles a day."

"That's Keith Moon. Moon the Loon. And you know he died, right?"

"Yeah. He drove his car into a swimming pool."

"He did do that, but I don't think that's how he died."

"Want some?"

Harold shrugged and took a shot. One of the other guys said that his older brother went to school with Harold and used to really like his band back in the day. He asked, "You guys got any shows coming up?"

"We're sort of looking for a new guitarist these days. Zach quit on us."

"Oh yeah, man," Matt said. "Zach's my guitar teacher. He knows, like, every Eagles song."

"Yeah, that's the reason we're looking for a new guitarist."

Maggie and Allison returned from the woods. They sat on the log with the guys and Maggie started laughing at something one of them said.

They finished their drinks and when Harold got back from the van with another Allison said, "We should get going."

"I just opened this," Harold said.

"We've got to get to the party."

Harold wanted to argue but then everyone else agreed. He got in the van and Matt got into the passenger seat; the girls sat in the back. Harold kept an eye on their whispering while Matt told Harold about how he was trying to learn the guitar solo from "Comfortably Numb" and asked him questions about gear.

They pulled up in front of a house with kids all over the lawn. Allison said, "Thanks, Dad" and jumped out the side door with the guys.

Harold said, "Hold on, Maggie. Can we talk a minute?" Allison stopped and Harold added, "*Alone.*" Allison waited for Maggie to say it was okay before she left. Harold turned around in the driver's seat and said to Maggie, who was still in the very back bench seat, "What's going on?"

"What do you mean?"

"I mean, I feel like you don't want me here."

Maggie looked out the window. She said, "Well, you're not really invited."

"No, I mean at all. Like you only want me to drive you around and pick things up for you." She didn't say anything, just stared out the window and bit her lip. He kept on, "It makes me feel used." He turned around and watched her in the rear-view mirror. She was still looking at the house. He said, "Why don't you just go."

She got out of the van and he did too, meeting her around the side. He said, "Look, I know your friends don't get us. They think it's weird. But it's okay, you know. You're a lot more mature than any of them."

He put his arm around her and walked toward the house. When they got to the front door, he put a hand on each of her cheeks and pulled her face into his. She opened her mouth a little bit, and he let a hand fall down to her chest. He stepped back and said, "Look, have a good time, okay."

Harold watched her go into the house. Matt came out. He said, "Hey man, you decided to come in. Cool."

"I was just going to head out."

"You should hang out, man. No one will care."

They went into the kitchen. Matt opened up cabinets until he found a bottle of vodka. He drank from it and asked Harold if he wanted any. Harold didn't see why not. He took a long drink.

Later, they were standing beside the stereo and Matt was saying that all the kids at his school listened to the same vapid, commercial bullshit and that people like him and Harold knew what music should sound like. Harold was mostly looking around the room for Maggie. Someone came over and asked Harold if he was a cop. Matt laughed and said, "No man. This is Harold. He's cool." Harold took another drink of vodka.

Then they were in the backyard and Harold was telling Matt about how much he liked Maggie and how he knew that she felt the same, but he always felt like Allison wanted him to go away probably because she was jealous or something. Matt was nodding and agreeing and telling Harold how rad he was and then Allison and Maggie came out the back door. Allison said, "What the fuck are you doing here?"

Harold said, "Matt invited me in."

"Yeah. Harold's my boy." Matt slapped Harold on the back. Harold nodded.

"Maggie doesn't want you here."

Harold asked her, "Is that true?"

Matt said, "You guys are wrong about Harold, he's cool!"

"Wrong about me?"

Allison said, "He means Maggie thinks you're a creep."

"She wouldn't say that."

"Tell him, Maggie."

When Maggie didn't say anything, Allison said, "She doesn't want to see you anymore."

"Is that true?"

"No, it's just…"

She didn't finish the sentence or look at him, but

everyone else was looking and listening. Harold said, "Come on, let's talk," and took her hand. He pulled her through the party and out the front door. She didn't resist much.

When they were past the last people on the lawn, near Harold's van, he spun around and grabbed her shoulders. "Is it true?"

And then Allison was there. She pushed Harold and said, "Get off her."

Harold ignored her. He opened the sliding door of his van and told Maggie he wanted to talk to her in private, and said to Allison, "Leave us alone."

Allison said, "No fucking way she's getting into your pervert van alone. She doesn't want to talk to you."

Maggie was crying. Harold took a couple of steps toward her and said, "Come on, we can talk this out."

He reached out for her, but Allison got between them again. He said, "I just need one fucking minute without you here, could you please just fuck off." Then, in a gentler voice to Maggie, "Come on."

Maggie finally looked at him. "No."

Allison said, "Told you."

Harold yelled, "Would you fuck off, you fucking cunt."

Allison punched Harold. She wound up way behind her back and followed through with all her weight. It was hard enough that Harold fell backward onto the ground. He sat there for a minute, then checked his nose for blood. Maggie pushed by Allison and asked if he was okay. He said, "I'm fine." Then to Allison, "Real fucking mature."

She said, "Whatever, I'm sixteen."

Maggie helped Harold to his feet. He pulled her close and said, "I knew you cared" into her hair. Then he held her at arm's length, looked into her eyes, and said, "I love you."

Maggie said, "I don't want to see you anymore."

Allison grabbed Maggie's arm and began pulling her toward the house. Maggie looked back at Harold and whispered, "I'm sorry." Allison smirked.

Harold stood alone in the driveway and watched the door close behind them.

Auction

Norm could tell the old lady standing in front of the hall was going to be trouble; there was no reason for her to be hanging around so early otherwise. He parked near the entrance and then made a great show of pouring a coffee out of his Thermos, sipping it, taking his time. He hoped she'd come over to him. She just stared at the truck, her hands up near her neck, wringing a handkerchief that looked like it had seen a lot of use.

Norm gave it a few minutes, then sighed and got out of the truck. He walked halfway to her and stopped, saying, "Viewing is at nine thirty, auction starts at ten. No early bids."

She took a few worried steps forward and said, "There's a violin. It was my grandfather's." Norm held out his hands, palms up, showing her there was nothing he could do. She took a few more steps toward him and said, "Please..."

When she got close enough, Norm slipped around her and jumped up the steps to the door. He stuck his key in and said, "I'm sorry, ma'am. That's the way it goes. You've got to bid on it like everyone else."

She was coming up the stairs, her hands back up at her neck, wringing her handkerchief. She said, "He wanted me to have it."

Norm said, "Nine thirty," and pulled the door shut.

The auction was already set up and ready to go, but Norm liked to show up early and go over everything before any of his crew got there. There wasn't much to do. He mostly just walked the rows of tables that were covered with everything from office supplies to collectibles, straightening and rearranging things that didn't need it. The stage at the far end of the hall was filled with furniture; he tilted some chairs to better catch the light.

It was a good collection. Sven, the executor of the estate, had told Norm that his deceased brother had owned a general store in town for decades and had held on to anything that didn't sell—toys, games and collectibles, and a whole lot of junk besides. On top of that, his brother had lived in the house the family had bought when they came over back in the 1880s.

Sven told Norm a long story about the aristocracy and angry peasants—the upshot of which was that the house had a lot of antiques from the old country. It was the sort of estate Norm only saw every few years: lots of genuine antiques and collectibles to go with the everyday home things. He expected a good turnout, even not counting the family, who, Sven had warned him, were going to turn up in force.

It seemed the family couldn't agree on how to divide everything; there had been no will and the relatives held mixed opinions on who had been promised what. Adding to the confusion, Sven said that, for as long as he could remember, everyone in the family had used the house as storage—anything anyone didn't want to keep but didn't want to throw away ended up there. Tracing what was whose among the four generations of children and uncles and cousins was almost impossible. Sven had spent a couple of weeks trying to sort it all out before he said to hell with the family—all trying to curry favour and politic for their own needs—and put everything up for auction. The family could bid on what they wanted, the rest would go to dealers, and he'd split the money earned amongst all the heirs—about thirty ways, he figured.

The lock clicked and the door swung open. Three of Norm's helpers came in, followed by Nancy, who handled the cash. She was trying to politely close the door while saying, "It will be there, don't worry. We're very careful with everything." She closed the door and saw Norm standing among the tables. "Did you know there's already someone out there?"

Norm said, "May have seen her. Something about a violin?"

Nancy laughed. "It's going to be one of those days?"

"I think so."

Nancy got the registration table set up with her laptop and cashbox while the guys checked Norm's microphone and the speaker set-up and made themselves look busy straightening the lots Norm had just inspected.

At nine thirty sharp, Norm opened the doors.

Before he could get the wedge under it, the violin woman was through the door. She gave Norm a reproachful look and then practically ran up and down the aisles, her head swivelling from side to side. An older gentleman Norm took for her husband followed her; he must have been hiding in the car when Norm pulled in. He nodded to Norm and followed his wife up to the stage, where she'd found the violin leaning up against an armoire. She held it close to her chest, eyes closed and sobbing. Her husband patted her shoulder, then went to the concession to get a coffee.

Norm greeted his regulars as they came in—the local antique and junk store owners, some private dealers—and he was pleased to see some of the bigger dealers from the city he didn't know as well; evidently word had got out. That was good. There were also some obvious looky-loos from the city hoping to experience a genuine country auction. And then Norm saw the overdressed folks he knew were the family. Families always wore their best, thinking an estate auction was some sort of continuation of the funeral. The regulars all wore jeans.

Norm watched as the ancient Sven trundled in guided by a cane, his hunch lost in a suit that was several sizes too big. He came straight to Norm and started in right away. "I suppose Hilde's been giving you a hard time?" He nodded to the woman cradling the violin. Norm grunted noncommittally. Sven continued: "She's okay, really. Just had a hard time in life, you know, never had much in the way of money, never a fair shake." He considered a moment. "Brought some of it on herself, I hate to say. She's always been quick to take offence, to think the world was out to get her." Norm let that hang in the air; he tried to stay out of family business. He was just there to sell.

Sven said, "Have you had the pleasure of meeting my other niece, Beata, yet?" He nodded to a woman who was bent over a walker that seemed to support her whole torso. Two younger relations held either elbow as she wheeled slowly up one of the aisles. Norm shook his head. "She is, as we like to say in the family, a real bitch."

Beata plodded past Hilde without looking at her sister, then turned down one of the rows. Every once in a while she'd stop and point at something, one of her children would hand it to her, and she'd hold it up close to her face, lifting her glasses to inspect it. She worked her way down the aisles while Sven explained to Norm how the sisters didn't get along—some feud supposedly over a piece of property, but actually over some boy back in high school. But even before that, they'd fought over things like combs and dolls. Beata was a big part of the reason he'd decided to go the auction route, Sven explained. Any time Hilde said she wanted a thing, Beata claimed their dad had said it was hers.

Norm greeted a few more regulars. Sven just kept on talking.

Beata walked by them and Sven said, "It's nice to see you, Beata."

She stopped and craned her neck up at them. She said, "Look at what you've done. All of our family history, laid out for these vultures." She looked at Norm. "How do you sleep at night?" The girl who held on to Beata's right elbow mouthed "Sorry" to Norm. He'd heard worse.

Norm watched Beata push herself away, her family in tow. Sven clapped Norm on the back. "I don't envy you today," he said. "Good luck."

All told, there were about two hundred people by the time ten rolled around. A good turnout, and more would trickle in as the day wore on. Norm grabbed the stepladder he used to get above the crowd and carried it down to the end of the first row. He climbed up and banged his gavel on its side to get everyone's attention. Then he turned on his little headset microphone, and after a blast of feedback, got things started.

He gave his usual patter about registration and the as-is rules, and then he added, "Now, I know you all love paying that buyer's premium, but we're waiving that today." That got some laughs. Since it had looked to Norm like the family would be bidding each other up, he'd offered Sven a flat fee, rather than his usual ten percent commission; it never felt right making money off a feuding family whose members were liable to drive the bidding up way over value. Which reminded him to add, "And I should also warn you all, this is a family sale. They're here and they're going to be bidding, so let me tell you, if you're bidding against family, you're not going to win." Most of the older dealers and regulars would bow out if the family were bidding—the polite ones anyways.

With his speech done, Norm got right into it. The first lots were the big, worthless things—filing cabinets, office supplies, chairs, boxes of unused paper. Norm started high, fishing, and then dropped the price down to move it along quick: "Do I hear a hundred for this here leather office chair. No? How about ten?" If no one bid, Norm added to the lot until someone was interested. Most of the stuff went to the indifferent junk store dealers; the early part of the auction was more to clear out useless things and give the latecomers a chance to show up than it was to make money.

He moved on to a table of kitchen supplies. Not the good silverware or anything high-end—the expensive stuff he saved for the end of the day. To start, it was just everyday items: boxes of cutlery, Tupperware, pitchers, plates, bowls, rolling pins, an apple corer. All the odd gadgets and Starfrit solutions that eighty years and three generations could leave behind. One of the antique dealers scooped up most of the lots for a few bucks a piece. After a stack of plates went to the dealer, Norm said, "And another lot to Phil. Trouble with the wife?"

The crowd laughed and Phil did too. He said, "Son's moving to the city for school."

"A scholar, like his old man," Norm said. "Maybe you can save us all some time. Twenty dollars for all the rest of the kitchen supplies here? Anyone object?"

Phil nodded; no one objected. Nancy wrote down the deal on the sheet while Norm climbed down the ladder and moved it toward the next set of lots. The spectators shuffled down the row with him. He climbed back up.

The next few tables were piled with toys, puzzles, and comics — an auction had to sell some stuff of value within the first hour or the crowd would turn. Norm started with the puzzles and games. All the lots had one good vintage box grouped with three or four new ones; lumping them together was a good way to move things that otherwise wouldn't sell. Once he got through those, there were the toys, about twenty boxes' worth, every lot divided up the same way — one or two collectibles mixed in with junk.

A few of the people Norm assumed were relations bid on some of the toys — a hobby horse, a set of metal cars, or a tin drum remembered from their childhoods — but the two sisters stayed out of things. Beata sat on her walker by the concession, her grown children gathered around her on folding chairs, and Hilde was anchored to the violin by the stage. Sven kept to the edges of the crowd, marking down prices and lot numbers on a sheet of paper. Norm tried not to think about the discussion of "errors" Sven was sure to bring up after the payout.

Norm worked his way through the tables while he and the crowd shifted down. As they neared the end of the row, one of Beata's children planted himself by the final table. Hilde's husband came over too. When Norm got close, Beata herself pushed her way over. Hilde stayed near the violin, but was standing up on the stage where she could see what was going on. Norm wrapped up the table he was selling and climbed down his ladder. The family didn't budge, and he and the crowd settled around them.

Sporting goods covered the last table in the row. Norm went through some fishing rods and tackle, and then a few boxes of old hunting magazines, sold by the lot for pennies. He kept an eye on the family, waiting to see what it was they were after. They all leaned in when his helper picked up a box of hunting knives to show the crowd.

"We better do this box by choice, folks," he said, figuring he might as well give everyone else a chance to get something. He reminded the crowd of the rules: highest bid gets to pick the item out of the box they want, then everything else goes up for bidding again.

Norm asked for twenty-five. Beata raised her hand. Hilde's husband went for fifty. Beata said seventy-five before Norm could ask for it. The crowd realized what was going on and sat back to watch. They went up by increments of twenty-five to two hundred dollars, and then Beata said three hundred. Hilde's husband looked back; his wife wrung her hands and Norm counted out slowly, going once, twice...then Hilde shook her head and Norm called it sold. Beata put the knife in her walker and pushed herself back to the concession.

Norm finished off the tables along the wall and led the crowd down the next row. One table had Elvis memorabilia, impressive looking, but mostly worthless. Then piles of sports stuff with a lot of Steelers gear. After that came another run of junk: cut glass bowls, "good" dinnerware—the sort that sat in glass cabinets and came out on holidays. It looked fancy but was all worthless. The crowd took the chance to head over to the concession a few at a time while Norm tried to get people interested. "Come on, folks, it's time you got into the fondue business," but he knew it was just a lull; there was always a slow stretch in the middle.

Near the end of the row, Norm announced he'd do the stage next. People trickled back. He climbed up past Hilde and looked out over the crowd. The whole family was there. Beata bent over her walker at the foot of the stage, Hilde on the other side. Sven smiled broadly up at Norm. The old guy couldn't wait for the showdown.

Norm sighed and reminded the crowd that the family would be bidding to win, and then he got started. Hilde and Beata got into it right away over a gramophone. Hilde bid first, but Beata won after it got near a thousand—way over what it would have cost at an antique store. Hilde raised her arms up to her neck and wrung her hands. She looked at her husband, who patted her arm.

A few lots later, Hilde tried again, this time for an oil lamp. Beata bid, impassively raising her hand after each higher bid until her sister backed down. They did the same thing over an oak table and a dresser and then an armoire—always Hilde acting first, jumping out with a bid, but Beata keeping in until she won. Sven got involved once, over a roll-top desk. He and the sisters went up to a thousand, and then Hilde dropped out. Beata didn't bid again either.

Norm realized Hilde was on a budget, not wanting to bid too high on anything so that she'd have enough for what she really wanted. He motioned for one of his helpers to bring the violin over, figuring he might as well give her what she was waiting for. He said, "I don't know a whole lot about violins, but this here looks like a good one. Do I hear a hundred?"

Hilde put up her hand; Beata said five hundred. The crowd collectively leaned in; the regulars knew they were about to get a show. Hilde pulled her hands up in front of her and wrung them. She said six hundred. Beata jumped to seven-fifty. After an eight-hundred bid it went to a thousand, then up by a hundred at a time from there. Beata called her bids right after Hilde, almost talking over her sister. Hilde got more frantic as they went up past two thousand, and then her voice seemed to give out. She'd just nod to Norm when he asked if she wanted to go a little higher. Then Beata would raise her arm and say a bigger number.

When it got up to three thousand, Hilde said to the ground, "You know I can't afford that," but kept bidding. At thirty-three hundred she said, "You got everything else. Why can't you let me have this?" Norm slowed down, gave Hilde a chance to think over her bids. At four thousand, she had tears in her eyes. She said, "Please, Beata, stop." It went up. Norm politely asked if she wanted to go to forty-five hundred. Hilde said yes and Beata said five thousand. Someone whistled. Hilde struggled, looked like she might go higher, then turned around and disappeared into the crowd. Her husband followed her as far as the ladies' room. Norm called it sold and Beata's son grabbed the violin off the stage and handed it to her. She laid it across the handles of her walker.

After a scene like that Norm knew there was no point competing with the crowd. They'd want a chance to talk it over, swap opinions, and remind each other of the craziest things they'd seen at auctions. Norm said, "Seems as good a time as any to take a break. I don't know about you, but I could use a coffee. See you all in fifteen minutes."

Norm climbed down from the stage and walked through the crowd to the concession. One of his regular dealers, a guy who specialized in musical instruments, followed him and hovered nearby while Norm added sugar to his coffee. He was smiling like he couldn't wait to be asked what he knew.

Norm looked around to make sure the family were out of earshot and obliged. "So, you miss out on something good there, Jim?"

The dealer laughed. "I wouldn't have given you ten dollars for it."

"That bad?"

"There's either a hell of a lot of sentimental value, or someone lied to them about what they had. It's junk, Japanese made, maybe from the early eighties." The dealer laughed, but Norm just shook his head. He'd seen enough folks lose money on bad information over the years not to find much humour in a scene like that.

"You're sure?"

"Not even five dollars, Norm."

And then there was some sort of trouble at the far end of the hall. Hilde was shouting loud enough to be heard at the concession: "...rolling over in his grave. You know Dad wanted me to have it." Norm walked over. Hilde's husband was holding on to one of her arms and the family were all crowded between her and Beata, who just stood there, bent over her walker with one hand resting on the violin. Two men Norm assumed were cousins were getting in each other's faces; Norm's helpers tried to keep them apart.

Norm whistled through his fingers; it was loud enough that everyone shut up. All eyes turned to him. "Look here, I'm trying to run a civilized auction. You two will have to sort out your problems on your own time, not in front of all these people."

Hilde turned to Norm, either on the verge of tears or just finished with them. She said, "Why wouldn't you let me have it?"

"I know it didn't go the way you wanted, but I just sell the stuff according to the law and the arrangement with the family. If you have a problem with each other, well, there's a barn out behind the hall you can duke it out in. But not here."

That got a laugh from the crowd, which calmed the mood a bit. Hilde's husband touched her elbow. She fell into herself, deflated, and was guided away. Beata said something that sounded non-complimentary and pushed herself back to her spot by the concession. As the crowd broke up, Norm saw Sven smiling broadly at him, pleased by the encounter.

Norm gave everyone a few minutes to calm down, then said to his helpers, "Might as well finish this up." He got back up on the stage and went through the last of the things there, but had trouble keeping the crowd interested. He had to keep banging his ladder to keep the murmur down, and by the time he got to the last row, the bidding had slowed and the crowd had started to thin out. Scenes like the one over the violin were enough for the looky-loos to leave feeling satisfied, and the dealers weren't as interested in the final lots. The last row of tables took as long as everything that came before.

By the time he finished the last table, the hall was almost empty. The family huddled in their groups around the hall; the dealers who had bought larger items were waiting by the loading doors for their turn to move their stuff out. A few regulars shook Norm's hand and let him know it was a good auction and then Sven was in front of him, grinning, and shaking Norm's hand. He said, "I'm real sorry about that scene earlier." He didn't seem sorry at all.

"I've seen worse."

"It's too bad though," Sven said. "You know, Hilde never had much money." Hilde sat on the edge of the empty stage, watching all the furniture being carted away. Beata sat by the concession, still holding the violin across the handles of her walker, watching her children carry out her other winning lots to a rented van.

Sven launched into more stories while Norm nodded to the folks heading out and shouted instructions at his helpers. Norm caught snippets: Beata had been quite a looker in her day, but had a taste for sweets. He heard again the story of the boy the sisters had fought over in high school. And then the full story of the properties Beata had inherited over her sister. "Because of her first husband, you see," Sven said, "she could hire a lawyer and hammer away. Hilde couldn't afford to fight it."

"Oh?" Norm asked in spite of himself.

There had been a cabin up north worth so little there weren't even taxes on it, but Beata had fought that away from Hilde. And there was a place in Germany that a distant cousin had owned; Beata ended up with that one as well. Then Sven was prattling on, talking about his dead brother and some old country feud that had led half the family to cross the ocean. Norm tuned him out.

He knew it wasn't his place to get involved in these sorts of things. It was important he keep it professional. It was no business of his who got what. But then he saw Beata had the violin out of the case and was making a big scene of cleaning some dust off of it right in view of Hilde, who was openly crying. Hilde's husband took her by the elbow and led her gently out the side door of the hall.

Sven had stopped talking to watch the scene with Norm. "Like I said earlier," he told Norm, nodding to Beata, who was putting the violin away, her point made, "a real bitch." Sven chuckled. "Got it from her mother, God bless, but she was a miserable one too…" Norm sighed and left Sven talking.

Norm went out to the parking and caught up to Hilde and her husband at their car. "Hold up a second," he said.

Hilde wiped her eyes and looked like she was trying to find some anger for Norm. Her husband patted her arm and said to Norm, "What can we do for you?"

"Can I ask you what's the story with the violin?"

Her husband answered, "It was her great-granddad's. He was a concert performer back in the old county. Apparently, it was made by some great violin maker. Hilde's dad taught her to play it when she was young."

"He wanted me to have it," Hilde said, barely audible. "Beata can't even play."

Norm was glad to hear that. "Well, I had a violin expert in today, and he seems to disagree with what you've been told."

Hilde asked, "What do you mean?"

"Look, I hate to be the bearer of bad news, but he said it's Japanese made. Maybe from the seventies or eighties."

"That's impossible. It's been in our family since I was young."

Norm held out his hands apologetically. "I'm just telling you what he told me. But I know how these things go; I've seen things like this happen before. Maybe someone sold it and replaced it without you knowing, or maybe it got broken and replaced. I don't know. But my guy knows his stuff—it's not what you thought it was."

"A fake?"

"It seems that way."

Hilde slumped forward, quick to accept another defeat. Her husband wrapped an arm around her shoulders and she said, without conviction, that she couldn't believe it. Norm looked down at the gravel, wondering if he should finish the thought for her. An awkward minute passed before she got there on her own. She stopped crying and looked up at Norm, eyes suddenly very clear. "You're telling me Beata just paid five thousand dollars for a fake?"

Norm nodded. "It seems that way."

Hilde blinked. "Well," she said. Then she laughed, a high, musical trill that she cut off almost before it began. She composed herself and said to Norm, "I thank you for letting me know."

Norm nodded and then she was looking past him and her smile turned into a glare. Norm looked behind and saw Beata slowly walking down the ramp out of the hall, helped by two of her children. He winced at the scene that sprung to mind—the sisters screaming, both blaming him. But Hilde seemed to sense his concern and said, "Don't worry. Your secret is safe with me." She laughed a little, and then said to her husband, "Let's leave that old hag to her garbage violin and go home."

They got into the car and started out of the parking lot, Hilde laughing and waving goodbye to Norm. He smiled and shook his head, and when he saw Beata looking confused, he decided it was time to go inside and help with the cleanup.

Low Risk

Ruth spent a long time thinking about it. A friend of a friend had mentioned that a friend of his up in the city was selling some candy machines for forty bucks a piece. They were an easy way to make money, he told her. You buy the machines, get the candy in bulk, and set them up around town. He was honest about no one having ever gotten rich with candy machines, but he thought it was a good way for someone to bring in a little extra cash.

Ruth was always behind. She raised three kids on welfare and picked up whatever under-the-table work she could as a cook. It never amounted to much, so she sublet the unfinished basement of their split-level rental out on the highway to keep her rent down, and her boyfriend, Tom, lived with them and helped out whenever he could—whenever he had work. Life was a struggle, and she always seemed to need money for some unexpected extra thing: a school trip for the kids or an unexpected repair on her old station wagon or some broken appliance in the house. The extra money brought in by the machines could be just the thing to take the pressure off.

Which was what she kept telling Tom, who just didn't think it was a good idea. They talked about it while she tried to get the kids away from the TV to eat their dinner and while she tried to get them to clean the dishes that they left behind so they could go watch more TV. As she slopped the leftover spaghetti piles into Tupperware, Tom asked why the guy who told her about the machines didn't buy them if they were such a sure thing. She figured it just wasn't worth the guy's time. He was making good money at the mill, what was a couple of hundred extra dollars? It was just a drop in the bucket for him. But for them, it could change a lot. "It could be the difference between eating spaghetti every night or having a lasagna every once in a while," she said. "Imagine what a little extra could do?"

Every time money came up, she'd bring up the machines again. When a faucet broke and they needed to scrape together ten dollars for a new one, Ruth pointed out how a little extra money would help.

When Tom had to patch a flat on his truck rather than a buy a new tire, she pointed out how a little extra money would help. When her youngest got hit in the face with a soccer ball and needed to see the dentist and she had to borrow money from Tom, she pointed out how a little extra money would help. Eventually, Tom had to admit that, at the very least, it seemed pretty low risk. It's not like the machines would lose value; if it didn't work out, they could sell them and just be out the cost of the candy. But he really thought she should have a few places lined up to take the machines before she shelled out any money for them. Ruth agreed he had a point.

She called a few friends. Norma, who worked at a garden shop out on the highway, said the guys there were always complaining about not having vending machines. That was enough for Ruth to ask Norma to ask her boss if she could set up her machines there. Norma wasn't so sure, but after a bit of pressing she said she'd see. A few calls later the answer came back. Norma's boss didn't see why not.

With her first customer lined up, she called the guy who had the machines. He told her they were actually fifty dollars each and he wanted to sell them all at once, so two hundred for the four. She didn't have that kind of money on hand. "Could you hold on to them for me for a little while?" she asked.

"No guarantees" was all he would say.

Ruth tried to get the money together. First from Tom, who said he couldn't help; he'd been driving without insurance for the past month because he couldn't afford even that. Her tenants weren't interested in loaning her money against the next month's rent, and any time she did scrape together a little extra it seemed to disappear into a hot lunch at the kids' school or some sports day or a spike in gas prices. Every time she came up short, Ruth thought how that extra couple of hundred a month would make these inconveniences less of a strain.

Every week she called the guy to make sure the machines were still there, always having to remind him of who she was and that she had called before. He would always say, "Oh yeah, sure," in a way that made it seem like he didn't remember her. But at least the candy machines were still there.

Her break finally came when one of the cooks at the restaurant she filled in at got sick for a week. She got enough extra shifts to have a bit of extra money for the first time in months. She drove up to the city to get the machines and was surprised when the directions took her to a warehouse out in the industrial part of town. She'd thought she was buying them from a regular guy, not a dealer. The front of the warehouse was set up like a pawnshop, with shelves and glass cases filled with electronics and kitchen gadgets and other junk. The guy sitting in a beat-up old recliner by the door didn't know anything about her calls, but seemed to think he'd seen a few candy machines in the back.

He led her through a gap in the shelves into the open back of the warehouse. It smelled of engine oil and mould. They walked through and over piles of paint cans and old car parts to a cold, damp corner with some old arcades and a half-built motorcycle. The candy machines were behind a pile of bike frames. The guy said, "This is them."

"They're a little more beat up than I expected," she said.

He shrugged and said, "I don't really know anything about them."

She reached over the bikes to feed a quarter into one of the machines. She gave the handle a spin; the crank inside where the candy would be spun at the same time. It looked like it worked. She asked, "Can I get my quarter back? I want to try the others."

The guy seemed put out, but went looking. He eventually came back with a key that opened the money collector. She pulled her quarter out and tried the other three. They all seemed to work okay, but without candy in them she couldn't really be sure. She asked the guy about that. He shrugged and said, "As is."

"Fifty seems a bit much. The paint is coming off and this one has a chip."

"Can't do anything about the price," he said. Ruth wasn't sure what her next move was; she'd hoped he'd haggle a bit. They stood there, both staring at the machines. He seemed to realize something more was needed. He said, "You know, these are the big industrial type, not the crappy plastic ones you find at kid stores."

On the drive home she went over the numbers again. She had tried to be conservative in her guesses about how much money they'd bring in, but she figured that each machine had to get at least eight spins a day; so, two dollars per machine per day. That was sixty dollars a month, times four machines, which was two hundred and forty. After the cost of the candy, which she'd pick up from the bulk store out on the highway, she was looking at six weeks until she turned a profit. That wasn't *too* long. And once she was turning a profit, she could finally pay for the things she had to tell her kids they couldn't do, and they could eat some decent meals every now and then. And if things went really well, she could use those profits to buy a couple more machines. She tried to keep her thoughts realistic, but she started imagining moving up to proper vending machines. Maybe even pop.

After she got home, she spent the rest of the day cleaning up the machines with a rag in the carport. One had some rust on the spinning thing inside that she hadn't noticed, but once the candy was on top, no one would see it.

When Tom got home from work he said, "Well, here they are." He spruced them up with some bright red paint. They stood together watching it dry and agreed the machines looked great. Tom said, "You might be on to something here." Her youngest asked if he could have some candy. She told him, for the hundredth time, no.

Ruth called Norma after dinner and let her know the machines were ready. Norma asked, "What machines?"

Ruth said, "The vending machines we talked about for your store, remember?"

"Oh, you got those?"

"Yeah."

"...I should double-check with the boss."

Ruth didn't see the point, since Norma had already talked it over with her boss and he'd said he was interested. And Ruth lived so close it was no problem to just pop by.

The next day, Ruth put on her best dress and carefully laid the machines on cardboard in the back of her station wagon. She put towels between them so they wouldn't bump into each other, and took the bags of candy out of the basement freezer where she'd hidden them. She had six different kinds: gumballs, chocolate almonds, Skittles, M&M's, jelly beans, and Reese's Pieces. She'd figured the guy might want to pick his flavours.

Ruth found Norma on the sales floor stacking hoses into a pile. Norma said, "You should have called. The boss isn't in today."

"Well," Ruth said, "I can just set them up somewhere."

"I really think we ought to check."

"I thought you had checked. Isn't it okay?"

"I ran it by him and he said it *could* work."

And then a woman was there telling Norma, "We need you to help unload the delivery once you're done helping this customer."

Ruth explained she wasn't a customer, and asked if she was the manager; as it turned out, the woman was the owner's wife, Gladys. Norma stared at the ground while Ruth explained how Norma had talked to the boss about the candy machines and how the guys wanted them and how he had thought it was okay if she set them up somewhere in the store.

Gladys looked at Norma, who said, "Well, he mentioned it could be okay."

Gladys said to Ruth, "No, we don't need those."

"But Norma ran it by—"

"Grown men can buy their own candy. Why would we want those?"

"Well..." Ruth hadn't thought she'd need to explain anything; it was supposed to be all set up. And now this woman was staring at her like she was wasting everyone's time and she felt like she had to say something. She looked around the store and saw an out. "There's lots of kids coming in here." She pointed at a toddler standing by a rack of shovels.

Gladys looked at the kid, considering. "So, what's in it for us? Why would we let you set up a machine on our property?"

Ruth hadn't thought of that either. She'd always just assumed that she could drop the machines wherever anyone would let her. But she felt like she was close. The woman knew there were kids, kids who wanted candy, and now she was waiting for a reason to put the machines in. Ruth said, "Well, it doesn't cost you anything." She knew that was the wrong thing to say as soon as she said it.

"No," Gladys said. "This whole place costs us something. We pay for every square foot. And we're not in the habit of just letting people make money off of it for nothing."

Ruth didn't know how to respond to that. She felt it slip away—the potential future money she thought would make things easier. It was like the woman was taking it all away from her. She felt a growing panic, but all she could say was, "I thought this was all okayed."

"We don't want them. Excuse me."

Gladys went back into the office and Norma said something about having to get back to work, leaving Ruth alone on the sales floor. She thought of following Norma, then thought about going into the office and trying again. She ended up just heading to her car, where she sat until she saw Gladys looking out the window at her. Ruth pulled onto the highway and headed home and put on the TV to take her mind off things.

That night, Tom asked why the machines were still in the back of the car. Ruth explained the whole thing to him, saying how Norma had led her on and how awful the owner's wife had been. Tom tried to be sympathetic, but at the end he said, "Well, it's no reason to start crying. It just means you've got to find somewhere else to set them up."

"But where?"

"Are you kidding? There's got to be a hundred places in town. Remember, you were going to expand to other locations anyways. This just means you have to look a bit sooner than you'd planned."

Tom set the kids in front of the TV and pulled out

the Yellow Pages. They sat at the kitchen table and went through the listings, underlining the addresses of likely shops, and then they made a list that started on the north side of town and ended on the south. The next day, after Ruth got the kids to school, she'd work her way down the list.

Tom lent her ten bucks for gas the next morning and she set off, wearing her best dress for the second day in a row, excited about her prospects. She even treated herself to a doughnut at the coffee shop on the south end of town. When she left, she saw four candy machines against the wall that she had never noticed before. She took them as a good sign—clearly some people were okay with vending machines being in their business. And it actually opened up a whole new line for her; she hadn't thought places that served food would want these machines.

She started at an industrial business complex with several shops just outside of town. The first place made trusses. Ruth wasn't too sure what those were but gave it a try. The manager was in and gave her a very quick "not interested"—no kids ever came into his shop and his guys didn't want candy. She tried the custom fabricator next door and got the same answer. The transmission shop, the ATV shop, and the custom carpentry place all said no. At the brake shop she was excited to see the manager was working his way through a bag of M&M's. "You can always have some on hand," she pointed out.

"But these haven't been sitting in a machine for five months."

"Well, it's only a quarter."

"For a handful. Sorry, I go to Costco and get a box for, like, twenty cents. I don't need a machine in here."

The last place in the complex was a cabinet maker. The nice old man who worked there said, "It's just me here now and I can't have sugar anymore on account of my diabetes." He smiled at her reassuringly and added, "I'm sure someone in town will want one of your little candy machines."

Ruth skipped the next few places on her list. They were all industrial shops outside of town, so she knew there wasn't much point wasting her time with them. She drove to the mall. There were machines by the entrance, which she knew about, but she thought that the toy store inside might be interested. As it turned out, they had their own machines. Theirs had toys and prizes in them as well—little plastic domes containing sticky hands, mini ring-toss games, stickers. She hadn't thought of any of that.

From the mall, Ruth walked down Main Street, popping into likely shops. She was surprised by how many of them had machines. Those that didn't weren't interested.

She went back to her car and started driving around. She figured the bowling alley already had machines but checked to be sure—they did—and then tried the laundromat next door. The guy at the wash-and-fold counter seemed interested, but then said, "I could just get one myself. What does one of those cost, like, thirty bucks?"

"They're more than that," Ruth said.

"Well, whatever it is, I'm sure I can afford it."

Ruth wasn't sure what to do with that. She didn't think it was fair for him to just go and get his own machine after she had given him the idea, but she knew she couldn't say that. Instead, she tried to think of a reason that he should go with hers, but when she couldn't she started to feel the same panic she'd felt the day before. She was so close—someone had been interested, even if it had only been for a second—and now she was losing the potential future money again. The wash-and-fold guy said, "Are you all right?"

Ruth said, "Thanks for your time," and walked quickly to her car.

On her way home she tried not to think about the money she'd wasted on driving around without managing to find a place for one of the machines. At home she made a sandwich and ate it at the kitchen table and went down her list again, first crossing off all the places she'd been and then crossing off the ones she'd passed by after deciding there was no point. Then she went through it again, crossing off the ones she figured wouldn't be interested. The list was a lot shorter, but there were still a dozen places. She thought about heading back out, but then turned on the TV and ate a few handfuls of M&M's and tried not to think about the money she'd wasted that day and how, if only the machines were out there, they'd be bringing in enough money that losing ten dollars wouldn't mean a thing.

She was warming up leftovers for the kids when Tom got home. She watched him get his tool belt out of the back of his truck and walk by her station wagon. He looked in the back and then headed up the deck stairs. He didn't say anything about it while they ate dinner and she didn't offer anything.

It wasn't until they were doing dishes that he asked, "No luck today?"

She shook her head.

"Well, there's always tomorrow, right?"

Ruth lay in bed that night thinking about tomorrow. She thought about how easy it should have been—the machines in a shop by the door, not in anyone's way; every few weeks she'd come by to refill them and take out the two dollars a day in quarters that was going to make things so much easier. And then she thought about all the people she talked to and all the ones she would talk to, and how they could just go buy their own if they really wanted to. She thought about how stupid she was not to have seen that before and she thought of how horrible that guy was for telling her it was easy money and how horrible Norma was for telling her there was a place for them and, finally, how horrible it was that she just hadn't thought the whole thing through properly.

After the house cleared out the next day, she tried to make herself go out and face it all. The panic returned; she replayed the conversations from the day before, knowing she'd have to hear the same things again if she went out. Instead, she put on the TV and watched whatever came on and tried not to think about money. The kids got home and started tearing around the house and then it was dinner and Tom came home and didn't ask about the machines.

It was the same the next day and the day after. Panic and anxiety kept her from going out, but whenever she went down to the station wagon, she would think about how she needed to find a way to make the machines work. And then she'd think about all the places she'd tried and about the money she'd wasted, and how spending more money to find a home for the machines was a waste, but then she'd think about how much the extra money would help.

After a week, she moved the machines out of the car and into the laundry room and then she didn't have to think about them quite so often.

A few weeks later she went looking for the candy and found that her kids had gotten into it, the empty bags buried in the bottom of the freezer. She screamed at them about how it wasn't just the cost of the candy they were out, but that they were out what the candy would have brought in and now she had to get the money together to get new stock and now she couldn't even find a place to put the machines because she had nothing to put in them. The kids laid low for the rest of the night, leaving Ruth alone in front of the TV.

Tom suggested one day that she try to sell them back; they were just in the way downstairs. She got mad. She still thought there had to be a way to make them work. She just wasn't ready to give up on the potential future money they could make. But she knew he was right. She called the guy who'd sold them to her the next day. He didn't remember anything about any candy machines and said, besides, even if they did come from his shop, he wasn't interested in buying them back. "They're a tough sell," he said.

Eventually, Ruth got tired of almost knocking them over every time she did laundry and moved them to the closet under the stairs, first in front of the Christmas decorations, and then behind, where at least she only had to think of them once a year.

"We Can All Be Happy"

The big fight happened in a small town a few hours north of the city. Doug and Larry were working a job there, laying block on a new strip mall. They and the other sub-contractors stayed at a motel during the week and drove home on weekends. When the job was nearly done, Doug and Larry decided to work through the weekend and save themselves driving back the next week.

After work on Friday they went out for dinner at the town's only bar—a windowless brick building with a steel double door that had "Pub" written over it. The bar was packed with the weekend crowd, the usual weekday drunks, and all the mill workers and family guys who didn't go out on weeknights. Doug and Larry had never seen the place so busy.

They picked up on the atmosphere of letting loose and decided to have a few more after they'd finished their dinner. They got pretty loaded watching a hockey game and then started cheering on the karaoke when it started after ten.

And then some lady was there, getting all over Doug. She danced up against him while someone screamed their way through a Hall and Oates song. Doug smiled at her and she ran a hand down his sleeve. A little cloud of concrete dust came off. She said, "I like a man who works with his hands."

Doug bought them all a shot and ordered another round of beer. A bit later, he did it again. Larry tried to ignore them. He turned his back to them but saw the woman straddle Doug in the mirror behind the bar. Finally, she went to the bathroom and Larry asked, "What's going on with that?"

Doug was pretty slurry by then. He said, "Hopefully something."

"What about Rhonda?"

"I haven't gotten any from her in years."

"I know." Larry took a long drink. He said, "She's a good woman though."

"Fuck her. She's a bitch."

"That's not fair."

Then the lady was back. More shots arrived and then Doug had her on his lap and a bit later they were messily mashing their lips together. Larry kept his eyes on a TV across the bar. Eventually, she went off somewhere again, and Larry said, "Jesus, man."

"What?"

"I mean, look..." Larry took a long drink of his beer and said, "This actually makes things easier for me."

"What easier?"

"Well, me and Rhonda, we've been seeing each other."

Doug put down his drink and said, "You serious?"

"She's been after me to tell you for a while. I mean, you guys barely live together anymore, and we both figured you had things on the side. We didn't think it would be a big deal."

Doug stood up. He said, "You piece of shit."

"We actually thought you knew already."

The woman was back. She wrapped her arm around Doug's and licked his neck. He shook her off and said to Larry, "You fuck."

The lady said, "What the fuck is your problem, man?" and pushed Doug. Doug straight-armed her away and swung his fist into the side of Larry's head. Larry went down and Doug fell on top of him. The lady screamed and then there were hands on both of them and they were dragged through the bar and kicked out onto the street.

Larry got up first. He flipped off the goons who'd dragged them out, then held up his hands when they asked if he wanted more trouble. They kept an eye on Larry while he helped Doug off the ground. He said, "We'd better clear out."

Doug shook off Larry's hand. "You fucker."

"Come on, let's go back to the hotel."

They walked up the street, past the town's single traffic light. Neither spoke, but when they got to the motel, Larry said, "Look, I got a case of beer up in my room."

"Fuck you."

"Come on, have a drink."

They went into Larry's room. Doug sat on the edge of the bed and Larry pulled two bottles of beer out of the mini fridge. He handed one to Doug.

"You fucker."

"You've been saying you're going to leave her for years."

"Fuck you."

"Come on, you know we had a thing back before you guys got together. I wasn't angry when you started going with her."

"You didn't fucking marry her."

Doug had already emptied his beer. He got another bottle out of the fridge and sat back down staring at the empty floor between his legs. "How long?"

"Not long. When you left for that job in the city. She found some lady's number in your pants pocket. I ran into her at the bar that night. We got to talking…"

"Fucking swine."

"You were seeing someone else, Doug."

"Doesn't matter. Rhonda's my wife."

"You don't treat her like one."

Doug got up and raised his fist. Larry put both his hands up. "Okay, sorry. Fuck." Someone banged on the wall over the bed. Larry said, quieter, "You got your hit in, man. I deserved that. But I honestly didn't think you'd mind."

"It's my wife, you fuck."

They drank their beers in silence. Doug finished his in three long pulls. Larry said, "Look, this could be a good thing. You guys get divorced. It won't be ugly. She won't sue or anything. The kids are old enough; there's no alimony. And she can come live with me and you can go fuck whoever you want without sneaking around. Just think about it. We can all be happy."

Doug looked at his empty beer, then up at Larry. "'We can all be happy'?"

"Exactly. See, it's not so bad."

Doug nodded. He went back to the fridge but didn't open it; he put his hands on top to steady himself. Then he noticed, on the small table beside the fridge, Larry's tools. The tape measure, a level, a hammer. He stared at them a long time.

Larry asked, "You okay, man?"

Doug said again, "'We can all be happy.'"

"Yeah, why not?"

Doug picked up the hammer, turned, and swung it at Larry's head.

How Nice It Would Be

Jen didn't recognize the email address mcalistercrowley @gmail.com. The subject line read, "In Town." She clicked it open.

> Hey JenJen, it's been too long, sorry I'm so crap at keeping in touch. I'll be back in town on Saturday and Sunday. Would love to see you. Brenda tells me you've got another kid. It'd be nice to catch up! Let me know if you're around. — Robert

Jen smiled. Robert McAlister. They'd been friends in high school, part of a group who spent most of twelfth grade skipping class and hanging around the only coffee shop in town. Robert left town the summer after graduation and had only come back once, to help his parents move. That was before she'd met Jack—at least seven years ago. Jen thought that couldn't possibly be right and went over the dates in her head. No, it had to be. She saw friends so rarely.

She thought, *Robert!* and smiled again.

The message said "Saturday or Sunday"; today was Friday. She clicked reply, but before she could write anything a xylophone started clanging.

Jen hurried out to the living room and pulled the mallets out of Bea's hands. She took the xylophone away too. Jen said, "You have to play quiet, your dad is napping."

Bea said, "Gwab," and stretched both hands out to her toys.

Jen said to Beck, "I asked you to make sure Bea stayed quiet."

Beck looked up from her drawing at the activity table. Her big eyes filled with tears. Jen walked over and crouched down over the little table and chairs. She hugged her daughter and said, "It's okay, I'm not mad. It's not your fault. I just need Bea to be quiet, that's all."

The ceiling creaked. Beck looked up and the baby said, "Ada ada da." Jen picked up Bea and rocked her and said, "Shhhh." There wasn't another sound from upstairs. After a minute, Jen put Bea back down and hid the loud toys. Beck went back to drawing, her face an inch away from her colouring book, trying very hard to stay in the lines.

Jen smiled at her daughter's tongue sticking out in concentration. She said, "Please, Beck, make sure the baby plays quiet." She gave Bea a stuffed duck and went back into the little closet that served as their computer room.

She wrote:

Robert! It would be great to see you. You should come out to the house, we live at 1412 Mountain Drive, out past Ronson's Corners. We're near where Dave Metham used to live, remember him?

She stopped typing. Robert would remember Dave; she and Robert had always made fun of him. A proud redneck living out in the boonies, he was the kid who drove a jacked-up pickup truck to school. He still had the truck—Jen heard it tear down the road every morning and night. And now she lived out here too. And the only vehicle she had was Jack's truck, which, she hated to admit, was also jacked up. She'd stopped thinking it was ridiculous years ago.

And her house was what they'd called a "redneck special" too. She leaned back and looked over the living room at the things she didn't notice anymore. The plywood floor covered with a worn rug that didn't quite reach the walls. The mismatched couch set, handed down from various family members. Fake-wood-panelled walls unfinished on one side. From where she sat, she could see through the two-by-four framing into the kitchen. Their only heat came from a woodstove in the corner of the living room. Wood was piled up the wall. Splinters made a path to the front door. Everything was half-finished or never started.

She deleted the message. It was almost dinner time; she'd write back later.

JEN SPOONED MASHED POTATOES into Bea's mouth while the baby slapped the tray. Beck said, "I don't like this."

"Well, it's what we're having."

Beck let her fork fall onto the potatoes over and over. Jen snuck a few bites of her own food while Bea chewed.

"It's gross," Beck said.

"No, it's not. It's potatoes. You eat them all the time."

"I'm sick of them."

"Well, try the meat."

"I don't like meat."

"Yes, you do."

"No, I *DON'T!*"

"Don't screech! Fine, you don't have to eat."

Beck put her chin on her hand and sighed. Bea stopped opening her mouth for food and swatted at the spoon instead. Jen wiped some potato off Bea's forehead and handed her a book to keep her busy while Jen finished her own meal.

The bedroom door opened upstairs. Footsteps crossed the floor, boots clicking, then silence. The toilet flushed. The stairs creaked. The front door opened and closed.

Beck said, "Where's Dad going?"

"He has plans tonight. You'll see him in the morning."

"Can I watch TV?"

"Sure."

Jen finished eating and then wiped Bea's face and hands, and dropped her back in the living room with her sister. She wrapped up the leftovers and did the dishes, then took stock of the kitchen. It was so hard to clean well, she hardly ever bothered. Jack had put in the linoleum tiles; the cracks between them filled up with grime that could only be cleaned out with an old toothbrush. The cabinets didn't quite connect with the floor—so, more grime there. A coat of grease covered the walls; Jack hadn't used kitchen paint, so any time she tried to scrub them, the paint smeared.

Beck said from the living room, "Mom, I'm hungry."

"Okay. I'll bring you something."

She'd just have to keep Robert in the living room if he came over. The kitchen was hopeless.

Jen sliced some cheese and put crackers on a plate. She dropped them on the couch beside Beck. Jen turned the TV down a couple of notches and then kissed Bea on the forehead. She decided to wait until the girls were asleep to see how tidy she could get things, then she'd write back to Robert.

It took an hour to get Bea down and then Beck wanted to hear stories again and again for an hour before she finally started to yawn. Beck fell asleep, and then Bea woke up. By the time they were both asleep it was late and Jen was so exhausted she decided she'd deal with the living room and her email in the morning.

JEN WOKE TO THE sound of the baby monitor crackling. She flipped over and turned it off. Jack was sleeping face down, away from her.

She went into the nursery where Bea was already standing in the crib. She smiled a wide-mouth, gummy baby smile and Jen smiled back. She swooped down to kiss the baby's head. She said, "I love you."

Bea said, "Ama ma."

"That's right, Mama."

She changed Bea's diaper and went downstairs. Beck was in front of the TV watching cartoons with the volume way down. Jen placed Bea on the floor and went to make coffee. Beck came in. "Mom, can we eat breakfast in the living room?"

"It's better to eat at the table."

"*Please.* I want to watch cartoons."

"We'll see…"

Jen stirred pancake ingredients together and got them started while she waited for the frozen orange juice to melt enough to mix it with water. She poured a bit of syrup on the pancakes and brought a plate out to Beck. She said, "Be careful not to spill any syrup on the carpet."

She made herself a plate and mushed up a few slices of pancake for Bea. They all sat on the floor together and watched cartoons. Jen mussed Beck's hair; she leaned away and said, "Muu-uum."

"I love you, Beck."

"Can I have more syrup?"

"There's enough on your chin to fill a bottle." Beck's tongue stretched down to find it.

The ceiling creaked. Jack came down the stairs. Jen stood up. He said, "We eat in the living room now?"

"I thought it'd be nice to have a picnic."

Jack walked into the kitchen. The cupboards opened and shut. The cutlery drawer rattled. Jen collected the plates and waited. Jack said through the door, "What's for breakfast?"

"I made pancakes."

"I mean for me."

"I could fry some bacon."

The fridge door opened, shut. "Are we out of cream?"

"I was going to pick some up, but you had the truck last night," Jen said. "I could go get some."

Jack said, "Don't bother. I'll grab something at the diner."

He came into the living room and pulled his jacket off the back of the couch. Jen said, "When will you be back?"

"Later. I'm going over to Don's to work on his car."

"Okay. I'd like the truck this afternoon. I need to pick up groceries."

"Give me the list, I'll get them."

Jen dropped the plates into the sink and pulled the list off the fridge. She added cream to the bottom and handed it to Jack. He crumpled it into his pocket and left.

• • •

JEN OPENED THE BACK door and tossed out the dirt in the dustpan. It was raining lightly. Heavy, low clouds hung over the house and the tops of the trees that surrounded it. The air was thick and cold compared with the dry fire heat inside. She watched the warmth from the open door push into the mist.

Beck had left a teddy bear out in their little square of yard between the house and the trees. Jen walked out onto the lawn, her feet sinking into the ground. She worried about all the rain; their basement always flooded. Everything down there was on cinder blocks, two feet off the floor, but even with everything safe, the flooding still caused mould. It needed to be fixed, but every time she brought it up with Jack he said it was fine, basements flooded. And they didn't have the money besides.

Jen wrung the bear out as best she could on the steps, then put it on a chair near the fireplace to dry. She went out to the half-finished carport to bring in more firewood.

She started the vacuum and Beck yelled, "Mu-um. Wait for a commercial!" Bea started crying. Jen turned it off until the program went to break, then quickly finished the room. She picked up and bounced Bea until she stopped crying. Then she dusted, cleaned the windows. Ran a cloth along the baseboards. When she was done, she looked over the room. It looked the same.

She went into the computer room and loaded her email. She wrote:

> So great to hear from you! Sorry for the slow response, I don't check email that often. But yes! It'd be great to see you. Maybe we could meet in town somewhere? I'll bring the girls. My number is:

Then she remembered: she didn't know when Jack was getting back. She deleted the message and looked at the blinking cursor. Did Robert know Jack? Jack had been a few years ahead of them in high school; Jen hadn't recognized him years later when he came into the hardware store where she worked as a cashier. Jack had said he remembered her. He'd asked her out the next time he was in the store. She'd said yes and now they had two kids.

Beck asked, "When's lunch?"

Jen made peanut butter and jam sandwiches for the girls. She got the leftover plate from the night before out of the fridge for herself. They ate in the living room again. Beck got bored of the TV and wanted to play. Jen put Bea down for a nap and then played a few games of Candyland with Beck while she thought of the best way to meet Robert. The house was out, and it was already afternoon and she still had no idea when Jack would be home. They'd have to meet the next day.

Jen put on a movie for Beck and went back into the computer room. She wrote:

Ack, sorry. Just got this. It would be great to see you—it's been so long. I suppose it will have to be tomorrow? Why don't you email me in the morning and we can plan something.

Then she deleted that too. She wouldn't know if she had the truck until tomorrow. She'd just email him in the morning.

JEN WOKE UP ON the couch. She'd fallen asleep watching late-night TV. It was off now; she half-remembered Jack coming in and telling her to come upstairs.

She made coffee and a piece of toast and went into the computer room. She tried to think of what to say to Robert. They could meet in town at the old coffee shop. She smiled and thought how nice it would be to hear him talk again.

Beck popped into the room and said she was hungry. Jen said, "Just a second."

Jack hadn't picked up groceries. She used the last of the pancake mix and added a handful of frozen blueberries she found in a balled-up bag in the back of the freezer. She went up and grabbed Bea from the crib and they all sat around the table. Beck told her a long story about a dream she'd had; there had been a bird and then she knew how to fly and their grandma was in it too. The stairs creaked. Jack came into the kitchen. He said, "Pancakes again?"

Jack started the coffee maker and then flipped a couple of pancakes onto a plate. He sat at the end of the table. Jen said, "Can I take the truck into town? I need to pick up some groceries."

"Sure, yeah. I need it at noon though."

"Okay."

"Can you take the girls with you? I want to get a couple of things done around the house."

Jen got the girls dressed and found their rain boots and got everyone out to the truck. Jack had taken the car seat out. She got Beck to make sure Bea didn't fall out of the truck while she pulled the car seat out of the carport and anchored it to the middle of the bench. She knew she should run in and write Robert, but Jack was in there and he'd ask what she was doing. It would be easier to stop at the library and try to get in touch there.

She drove carefully down the driveway; it was all potholes. One had gotten so bad she had to pull into the underbrush to avoid it. Branches scraped along the side of the truck and then they bounced onto the road, which was still dirt but a little bit better. Ten minutes on that road took them to the highway into town.

The library was closed; it was Sunday. Jen said, "Fuck."

Beck said, "Bad word!"

"I know, sorry." She drove back to the shopping centre out on the highway and put Bea in the cart and told Beck to hold on to the side. They went up and down the aisles, Jen dropping things in and taking out what Beck tried to sneak in.

She wondered where Robert was staying. There probably wouldn't be much reason for him to come to the grocery store, but she lingered anyways; it would be nice to bump into him. She didn't drive home right away either. Instead, she pulled into town and drove down Main. It had been a long time since she'd gone downtown; she mostly stuck to the shopping centre out on the highway. There were new shops everywhere. She was surprised to see a record store, and thought she should check out the new scrapbook store sometime.

She drove by the old coffee shop where she'd spent most of her later school years. Maybe Robert had thought of checking it out himself? She saw the owner through the window, looking exactly the same as she remembered. A bunch of teens were sitting out front, and a few old guys she recognized as the same old guys who had hung out there when she was a teen. She'd thought they were ancient back then, but they must have only been in their forties. Not so old-seeming anymore.

Beck said, "Mom, what are you doing?"

"Oh, nothing. Just driving around."

"I'm bored. Can we go home?"

"Sure."

But she took another pass through town, enjoying just driving, looking at the town, not rushing home. She knew it was silly to think she'd run into Robert, but she thought, again, how nice it would be if she did. After a loop through the park where she and Robert used to go when they skipped school, and a quick drive-by of the community centre some of the boys used to skateboard behind, Jen got back on the highway and headed home.

JACK WAS STANDING ON the front step when she pulled in. She unhooked Bea from the car seat and got out, holding the baby between her and Jack. He said, "I told you I needed the truck at noon."

"I know, it just took a while."

"Two hours?"

Jack stepped forward; Jen stepped back. Jack got into the truck and slammed the door. Jen balanced Bea on her hip and pulled the groceries out of the back before Jack backed out. He turned around and revved the engine on the way out. A black cloud of smoke lingered over the driveway. Beck walked though it and said, "Where's Dad going?"

"He's got to visit some friends. Come on, let's go in the house."

She dropped Bea on the floor and picked up the dish Jack had left on the coffee table. In the kitchen, she loaded the groceries into the fridge and made the girls lunch, then turned on the TV for them. She kissed the top of Bea's head and ruffled Beck's hair. Beck said, "Mu-uuum," and leaned away.

Jen went into the computer room and turned on the computer. She wrote:

Hi Robert, Sorry I missed this. I don't check email very often. It would have been nice to see you though! Let me know next time you're in town?

She looked at what she'd written and then deleted it all. She turned off the computer and went into the living room to play with her girls.

Fernando's

A friend told Jeff that he knew someone who was a sous chef and needed a dishwasher at her work. Jeff got the address, and the next afternoon printed out a resumé at the copy shop on the corner that charged four cents a page. He paid with a quarter, got his change, and headed over to the restaurant.

Fernando's was a fine dining establishment in an old character house. It wasn't open yet, but there was a waiter laying down the tables in one of the private dining rooms. He led Jeff back to the kitchen.

Mary looked at the resumé while Jeff explained their connection, which, he realized, was just some guy. She said, "Can you start today?"

"Like, now?"

"Yeah."

"I guess."

"Let me run it by Concepcion. She's the head chef." Jeff realized there was another person in the kitchen, a small woman behind one of the floating counters. Mary said, "Dishwasher?" and pointed at Jeff.

Concepcion said, "No, no, no."

"I need help. I can't prep and cook and wash dishes and do everything else around here."

Concepcion said, "No, no," and put her hands on either side of her head, shaking it.

"Come on. It's a Friday, I'm going to be slammed. I need the help."

She swooshed her hands downward. "Ask Fernando."

Mary said to Jeff, "Fernando will be in in an hour. Get started—I'm sure it will be okay."

Mary handed Jeff an apron and he went to the dish pit. There was a dish rack, a deep sink with an overhead faucet on a boom, and space to slide the dish rack into the washer.

There were three racks, enough to keep things moving. Two racks were already full of dishes and the sink was overflowing with pots and pans soaking in dishwater. He tied on the apron and got started.

An hour later, Fernando was pointed Jeff's way. He asked, "You work hard?" and when Jeff nodded, he said, "You need to go quick quick quick in the kitchen." Jeff nodded again. "Okay, good. I pay six an hour, cash, every shift. Waiters tip you out."

Six dollars an hour was two dollars under minimum wage, but Fernando explained that, if Jeff were getting taxed on minimum wage it would work out to be less than six an hour, so he was actually paying Jeff more than minimum wage, if you thought about it. And tips would make it even more. Jeff had worked in enough restaurants to know the deal.

THE SHIFTS STARTED SLOW. Prep work for the evening and a bit of cleaning. Mary got sauces ready between smoke breaks, and Concepcion talked to herself in Spanish and slammed things around. Jeff noticed she was often angry and always asking if anyone had seen Fernando, who usually arrived a couple hours after everyone else. After a few shifts, Jeff asked Mary what was up with that and she told him, "Oh, Fernando has a girl he sees before we open," and when Jeff looked blankly back at her, she added, "Fernando and Concepcion are married."

Jeff said, "Ah."

The waiters showed up around 4:30 p.m. On weekends, there were two of them, but otherwise Fernando tried to get away with having just one. The waiters took orders and bussed their own tables while Fernando, when he finally showed up, greeted customers and checked in on them. These check-ins were mostly a chance for him to drink wine and tell stories.

One of Jeff's jobs was to shine the copper pans. They were a big part of the presentation of Fernando's scampi dish; the shrimp were cooked in sauce, arranged in a spiral, covered with garnish, and then served in the still steaming pan. Fernando wanted those pans to "shine shine shine" when the scampi was served.

After scraping off the stuck-on burnt bits and cleaning the pans by hand, Jeff had to polish the outsides using a chemical foam that left the copper shining and streak-free. Because the chemical was so harsh, he had to wear different gloves than he used in the dish pit, but things happened so quick that he just did it without any gloves at all. Once clean, he'd hang them near Concepcion's station, but more often he would have to hand them right to her. She spent half the shift shouting, "Pans! Pans! Why are there never pans?" or, "I need the pans. Pans, pans, pans!"

There were only eight copper pans to go around.

When they were out of copper pans and had a scampi order to fill, which happened whenever it was busy, Concepcion cooked the scampi in a regular pan and left it on simmer until a copper pan was free. She'd yell at Jeff, who would ask the waiters if anyone was done with theirs, and the waiters would tell Jeff it was such bullshit that Fernando didn't hire a busboy or just let Jeff go out on the floor. And Jeff would tell Concepcion that it would be a minute while she shouted "Pans pans pans" at him.

When a pan became available, Concepcion would put it on her pass-through and Jeff would spot clean the sides with the toxic cleaner to remove any burn marks or scuffs. He'd try only to touch the pan with the cloth because it was always hot from the fire but he'd often miss and burn his fingertip. Sometimes Jeff got busy and wouldn't notice the order was up and one of the waiters would take it away, and then Fernando would come back in with the scampi pan seconds later and say, "You send it out like this?"

And Jeff would say, "I was about to clean it."

And Fernando would say, "You need to be quick quick quick if you want to get ahead," and Jeff would wipe the sides while Fernando tapped his hand against his thigh and repeated, "Quick quick quick."

Scampi was their most popular dish.

ERIC, ONE OF THE WAITERS, stuck his head into the kitchen and said, "Where the fuck is Fernando?"

Concepcion said, "He is worthless," and some other things in Spanish.

Mary said, "I'm going out for a cigarette."

Jeff said, "He's out."

Eric pulled the table cloths out of the linen closet to dress the tables. He said, "This fucking bullshit. What sort of place doesn't have busboys to do the set-up?" He put the pile of linen down and said to Concepcion, "What the fuck?" Concepcion raised both hands and shooed Eric away.

Eric set the tables and shouted through the pass-through, "I mean, I can't do this alone. I told him that. He wants one waiter. He doesn't have busboys. I've never seen anything so poorly run. Twenty-five years in fine dining, I've never had to do half the shit he expects me to…" Jeff started the dishwasher and drowned out Eric's complaining.

When the machine finished, Eric was saying, "…in Düsseldorf. And that's not all. I'm talking to a gallery in Paris, one in Rome. They want me, man." Eric liked to talk about his art career, which he felt suffered from all the hours he had to spend waiting tables. Eric said, "Fuck. I don't need this. He needs me, not the other way around."

Eric put on his tie while Jeff waited for another load of dishes to come out. Mary came in and mixed some sauces, then went out for another cigarette.

Concepcion sat on a small stool, shaking her head. Fernando was not in when they opened.

Eric greeted and sat the first customers, then came into the kitchen and said, "This is a fucking joke. This is supposed to be fine dining and you run it like a fucking Arby's. Worse — at least an Arby's would have a decent fucking manager."

Concepcion waved and said, "Go away."

Eric went into the bathroom. A minute later he came out and said to Jeff, "So, you're just going to stand there?" Jeff had started to notice that the coke tended to bring out the worst in Eric. There were no dishes. The pans were all shined. Mary was out back having a cigarette. The only thing left to do was take the orders. Eric said, "Fuck, it's always like this. Fernando ditches me on these fucking shifts and not one of you fucks is going to help me."

Concepcion said, "Go wait tables and leave us alone."

"Get your fucking husband back here."

"You don't talk to me like that. I own the place."

"Then hire more staff."

"You shut your mouth."

Jeff picked up a pan and started shining. Eric left and came back a minute later. He said, "Two scampi." And then, "They're not even drinking. Cheap fucks. The tips won't even be worth my time tonight."

Mary was back and another couple showed up, and then a group of four. Eight diners were enough to keep them all busy. Jeff fell into scrubbing, loading, shifting, shining. The night went by quickly.

Eric came in when there was just one table left and said, "This is a fucking joke. They didn't even order a dessert. What kind of fucking date is that? Cheap fucks. And you"—he rounded on Concepcion—"I'm doing this whole thing myself. Where's your fucking husband?"

Concepcion said, "Be quiet. I don't know where he is." And she put her hands up on her head and went to the office upstairs.

The last table left. Eric looked at his tip and said, "Ten percent—are they fucking German?" and tore off his tie and left without tipping out Jeff. Mary collected the last of Concepcion's dishes and her own. Jeff took out the garbage while the last load was running. Concepcion had left. Mary waited around for Jeff to finish mopping and then locked up.

THE NEXT DAY, FERNANDO came into the kitchen while Mary was doing the prep work. Jeff picked up a clean pan and scrubbed. Fernando had garlic in a plastic bag. He said, "Use this tonight. It's from my garden."

Mary took the garlic and said, "I already did the garlic. I don't have time to prep this."

Fernando said, "No time? No time?" His face turned red. "You prep it like I said."

Mary said, "I'm busy."

Concepcion said, "Leave her alone, Fernando. She's busy."

Fernando said something in Spanish. Then he turned to Jeff. He said, "Jeffrey. Here, I'll show you." Jeff came over. Fernando said, "You see, it's from the garden. You ready it, like this." He banged each bulb with a flat knife so it broke apart. Then he peeled one clove. "When I started out, I prepped the garlic every day. Big place. Hundreds of tables. For three hours I did the garlics and then I got so good I do it in an hour and a half. Then they made me sous chef. You work, quick quick quick, you'll make it big in this business." Fernando gestured at the building, in general. He smelled of wine.

He watched Jeff break a bulb, then peel a clove. He said, "No no no. Like this," and peeled a different clove. Jeff tried to mimic his movements. Fernando said, "No no no," and peeled another. Jeff tried again. Fernando said, "Good." He did a few more with Fernando watching closely. When there was enough, Fernando had him mince it. He said, "Good. But you must do quick." Jeff waited for it;

Fernando added, "Quick quick."

Concepcion said, "Get to work, Fernando. Leave the boy alone."

"Shut up. I'm helping him. He won't be a dishwasher his whole life. I help him get skills. Then, maybe, a better job. Money." He elbowed Jeff in the ribs and said, "And then, maybe, better women," and winked. Concepcion started yelling in Spanish.

Fernando waved his hands at her and said more in Spanish and left.

Mary stepped over to where Jeff was peeling the garlic and pushed it all into the garbage. She said, "It's all shit, rotten. He's always trying to pull this crap."

She went to the fridge and pulled out her prepped garlic. She sat it on the side of the prep area and told Jeff to get to the dish pit while she went out for a smoke.

A few minutes later Fernando came back. He said, "You did it all?" He held up the container. "Quick quick quick!"

FERNANDO CAME INTO THE kitchen juggling four hot scampi pans. He said, "No no no. Scuffs. See? It must be clean. This represents us. It is my signature dish."

Before Jeff could grab a rag, Concepcion said, "Your signature dish? *My* recipe. You are nothing without me, but you go out and you see that..." She switched to Spanish. Jeff had learned that *puta* meant slut. The rest he could piece together.

Fernando went upstairs to the office. It was an hour before Jeff saw him again. He came into the kitchen and said to Mary, "The diners like your Gambas al Ajillo; they say it's the best they've ever had."

Concepcion slammed a dish and threw it across the kitchen. It bounced off the wall and into Jeff's dishwater. Steam shot up. "You crazy woman!" Fernando shouted. Then to Jeff he said, "Ignore the women. They're all crazy."

Fernando was loaded.

Fernando left. A minute later, there was a pop and applause. He was comping champagne to the customers.

Eric went into the bathroom for the length of time it took to do a line of coke and then came into the kitchen. He said, "That shit wants to give away booze after leaving me on my own for the last hour, he can do the fucking cleanup himself." He grabbed his jacket out of the closet and added, "I don't need this. I've got a gallery interested in representing me. In Paris." He added: "France."

Jeff started a load of dishes and looked out of the pass-through. The last two tables were beside each other. Fernando stood between them, slopping champagne on the ground while he mimicked swimming. The diners' dishes were un-bussed. The dishwasher stopped. Jeff unloaded it.

Concepcion had left. Mary said, "We might as well clean what we can." And they started doing all the pots and pans and shutting down for the night. When they were almost done Fernando came in and said, "Scampi, four orders." And left.

Mary said, "That fuck."

They couldn't find Concepcion so Mary had to fire up the oven and pull out all the pans. She warmed some old rice and garnishes. She hit the bell. And again. And once more. Then Fernando was in the kitchen saying, "Where is Eric?"

"He left," Mary said.

"Left? Left? Left? We still have tables." His face turned redder. He asked, "Where is Concepcion?"

"She left."

"Who made this?"

"Me."

"No no no." Fernando looked at the dishes. "It's all wrong." He started arranging the shrimp with his hands, licking the sauce off his fingers. He opened the fridge and pulled out some sprigs of parsley while telling Mary it was "wrong wrong wrong." Fernando left with the copper pans unshined. He was even drunker than Jeff thought.

Mary took off her apron and said, "I can't handle this. Do you mind if I take off?"

"Go for it."

Jeff cleaned all the dishes he could and then tried to go out to get the dishes that were left on the tables. Fernando said, "No no no," and shooed him back into the kitchen. Jeff gestured at the plates. Fernando said, "Back of house staff stays in the back."

"I know. I just need to clean up."

"We have tables. Wait. You never rush customers. They are here for a good time."

They left an hour and a half later.

Jeff collected the dishes and scraped off the remaining food. Fernando leaned in the doorway and said, "You are good. Good worker." Jeff loaded the rack and pushed it into the machine. Fernando talked while it ran; Jeff didn't hear anything until, "...Eric. He's entitled. Thinks the world revolves around him. And Mary. She doesn't care. But you"—Fernando slapped Jeff on the back—"you didn't abandon me. You're hard worker. Like me."

Jeff got the mop bucket and filled it with water. Fernando leaned on the doorway and stared at nothing. Jeff dipped the mop in the bucket and started cleaning. Fernando said, "I started like you. I was nothing. Just a poor nothing. No prospects. No skills. Nothing. And I had to clean a kitchen. It was big. Not like this. Industrial, you know, for making lots of food."

Jeff lifted the mop bucket over the sink and dumped it. Fernando said, "Three years I worked there before they let me wait tables. They make you learn. They make sure you are serious. Are you serious?" Jeff shrugged while he mopped. Fernando said, "Jeffrey. Are you serious? About this." Fernando gestured around the empty kitchen. Jeff nodded as firmly as he could manage. Fernando said, "I can tell. You are good. You stayed. Loyal. Work hard. You will be like me one day." Fernando thumped his chest, then slapped Jeff on the back.

Fernando left the kitchen. Jeff took out the garbage and came back in. He couldn't find Fernando anywhere. He double-checked the office and all the rooms. He left the back way, so the door could lock behind him.

JEFF GOT TO WORK and saw a notice on the door. It said Fernando's Fine Dining Restaurant was in arrears to Global Real Estate LLC and had been evicted by order of the city bailiff. The door was padlocked.

He was wondering what to do when Mary showed up. She said, "Those fucks. Those absolute fucks." She lit a cigarette. There were tears in her eyes. "They said this wasn't going to happen. Fuck." She kicked the door. "They're a month behind on my pay."

Jeff said, "A month?"

"You too?"

"Fernando paid me cash." Jeff added, "Sometimes."

"Those fucks."

Mary pulled out her phone and tried calling Fernando. It went straight to voicemail. She had Jeff try on his cellphone. "They know my number," she said. It didn't even ring; they must've turned off their phone. Mary said, "What am I supposed to do? I have rent."

She pulled on the padlock, flipped it up in her hand and let it drop. Jeff walked around the side of the building. Mary followed. The back door was padlocked too. Jeff climbed up the fire escape to the second floor. The fire door was locked. He tried a window but it was locked. Then he stepped over the railing onto the roof and crouch-walked over to the next window. It slid open. He went in and the motion alarm went off. He walked around and unlocked the window beside the fire door. Mary climbed inside.

They went down to the front door and Mary punched in the alarm code. The phone rang. Mary picked it up and said, "Yeah, sorry. I was tangled up with some food and couldn't get to the keypad in time... Yeah, the password is 'Scampi'... Thank you."

Mary went into the linen closet and reached up above the top shelf. She pulled down the coffee mug with the float in it and dumped it onto one of the tables. There were two twenties, a lot of smaller bills, and change. It was just under a hundred bucks. She started to divide it and Jeff said, "You keep it—I got paid more recently."

"You sure?"

"Yeah, I got enough for rent."

"Thanks." She put the cash in her bag and then they heard a banging at the door, followed by thumping. They stepped back so they wouldn't be visible from the window. Eric looked through. Mary and Jeff both froze. Eric had his cellphone up to his ear. They could hear him saying, "Fernando, you piece of shit, pick up."

They didn't discuss letting him in or giving him any money.

They heard Eric try the back door, then the upstairs fire exit. They waited until they saw him cross the street before they started moving around again.

Mary got a box from the supply closet and took it into the kitchen. She loaded it with supplies. Pans, pots, cooking implements. She said, "This shit is expensive." Then she looked around some more. She said, "I wish I had a car. There's enough here to start my own place." But she had to settle for what she could carry. She offered Jeff a couple of pans—"You can probably get thirty bucks for these online"—but Jeff said no. She put the box at the top of the stairs, then went into the walk-in fridge.

Mary filled up her bag with blocks of cheese and shrink-wrapped meat. Jeff took a few blocks of cheese for himself and some frozen soup. They went into the basement together and raided the wine cellar. Mary fit three bottles into her bag and carried two more in her hands. Jeff couldn't juggle the cheese and wine and soup. He went upstairs and grabbed a table cloth that he folded into a sack. It was awkward, but he got a dozen bottles in it, on top of the cheese and soup.

They went back upstairs and left through the fire exit. They walked together along the back alleys until they were sure they were far enough not to be seen with their loot by anyone who might care.

When they reached the main street, Mary said, "I'm going to hop on a bus and get this shit home." She put her box down and gave Jeff a hug. They exchanged numbers and promised to call each other if either heard of any job openings. Jeff slung the table-cloth sack over his shoulder and regretted not grabbing a corkscrew.

Drive

Colleen and her sister Janet sat in a booth near the back of the bar. Colleen's fiancé Kevin was at the bar buying a round for his crew. They cheered and tipped back their glasses and then spread out. Greg came straight to the booth and pulled Janet up to her feet. She half-heartedly told him no and then they were out on the dance floor. Colleen sipped her Coke.

She hadn't wanted to go out. Kevin's crew had just wrapped up a three-month job and she knew it was going to be like this — all the trades drinking away Kevin's money. Her sister had made it a big deal though. "Come on," Janet had said. "You have to go."

"Why would I go just to watch everyone get wasted?"

"I need you to be there. Greg will be there."

Colleen didn't like Greg and hadn't from the moment he'd shown up at their door six months ago claiming to know Kevin's older brother. Kevin was a soft touch with anyone from back home, so he'd hired Greg and let him stay at their house until he found his own place. Janet was living with them. She was only eighteen but their parents had kicked her out of the family home when they found out she was dating a high-school teacher—not one of her own teachers, at least, but it was after she'd already been engaged to a biker, and had a pregnancy scare with a different man. Their parents had had it with the scandals and sent her packing. Colleen and Kevin needed help with the mortgage, so it didn't seem like too much trouble to take her in. Greg started moving in on her right away.

Colleen hadn't liked that; she tried to talk to Janet about it but the conversation ended quickly—"Who are you, *Mom*?" she'd said—so instead Colleen insisted that Kevin tell Greg to find his own place. He moved in with some of the other guys on the crew but still hung around their place all the time, picking Janet up from work, bringing over food; Colleen just couldn't get rid of him.

Colleen watched Greg loom over Janet on the dance floor. He was quite tall, dark-haired—Colleen could admit he was good-looking. But Janet still looked like she was too young to be in bars, which she was, so together they looked almost like father and daughter. Janet practically had to look straight up to kiss him. Colleen tried not to watch.

She had tried over and over to explain to Janet why Greg was a bad match, but it was impossible to get anywhere with her younger sister. If Colleen pointed out how there was no way to rely on Greg—he had no connections there and could up and leave without any notice—Janet would point out that Kevin had been in a similar situation when he first got to town. If Colleen said Greg was too old, Janet would say he wasn't much older than Kevin. If Colleen tried to explain the deeper problem, it would never come out right. She'd struggle to find words and end up saying that Greg was just...*creepy.* That always turned the talk into a proper fight.

Her sister was quick to anger—a full-body, shaking rage, just the same as when they were little kids. She'd scream that Colleen was just jealous because Greg was such a handsome guy and that she didn't want Janet to be happy because she was so fancy with her rich, successful fiancé. And all she wanted was to be happy. And then she'd say that Colleen was acting just like their parents and storm off to her room, slamming the door.

It was always like that with Janet. She'd cool off and everything would be forgotten a few hours later, but the fights stuck with Colleen; she'd have kicked her sister out if she hadn't known Janet would just move in with Greg.

Kevin slumped into the booth beside Colleen and threw an arm around her. "Havin' fun?"

Kevin was already bleary-eyed, trying to focus. Janet came over dragging Greg by the hand. Greg winked at Colleen and sat down.

The waitress came by with three pitchers someone had ordered. Kevin reached into his pocket and unrolled a wad of twenties and all the crew came over to top up their drinks.

An hour later, after refusing Janet's attempts to get her out on the dance floor and turning away Kevin's sudden affection, Colleen was still sitting there. Kevin had passed out; five beers was enough to put him under for the night. When Janet came back to refill her drink, Colleen said, "We really should get out of here."

Greg came over. He elbowed Kevin in the ribs and asked about another round. Colleen said, "I think everyone's had enough."

Greg said, "Come on, we're having a good time." He elbowed Kevin again, "You got one more in you, right?" Kevin barely opened his eyes but reached into his coat pocket and handed over some cash.

Colleen said, "I don't think..." but Greg was

already up at the bar. He ordered shots for everyone and then, right after, two more for him and Janet. Colleen tried to climb over Kevin, but he was suddenly awake again and pulled her down for a sloppy kiss. She managed to get to her feet. Kevin passed out again. Colleen went up to Janet and pulled her away from Greg.

"We'd better get out of here, it's getting rowdy."

"Come on, it's just getting fun."

"We have to go. Kevin's passed out."

"Greg's our ride. I don't think he wants to go." She called Greg over. "Colleen thinks we should go."

"Come on, Sis, have a drink, let loose." He slapped Janet's ass; she yelped and then fell into him a bit. He winked at Colleen and said, "You should be more like Kevin. He knows how to have a good time."

"He's passed out."

"Second wind." Greg pointed at Kevin, who was bouncing his way through the tables in the direction of the bathroom. Colleen went after him to make sure he was okay.

She waited outside the bathroom a long time and finally had to get one of the crew to go in and make sure Kevin was still alive. They got him back to the booth and then another round of pitchers appeared in front of them. The waitress came to Colleen looking for payment. She sighed and pulled out Kevin's wallet.

Greg and Janet came over to refill their drinks and then Janet excused herself to go to the bathroom. Greg sat down across from Colleen and said, "What's your problem anyway."

"No problem. I just don't like being out at bars that much."

"Or is it me you don't like?" His face was dark, eyes focused and unfocused while his hand searched for a drink. Colleen leaned into Kevin and jabbed him in the ribs. He only grunted. Greg said, "You've got a problem with me."

"It's not that."

He leaned over the table. His breath smelled like whisky and cigarettes. He looked like he thought he was making a point when he repeated, "You've got a problem with me."

Colleen said, "I just don't think you're good for my sister."

Then Janet dropped down into the booth. Greg stared darkly across the table at Colleen while her sister said they should get another drink. Greg and Janet stood up and went to the bar. Colleen tried to get Kevin up without any luck. When she gave up, she saw that Greg was staring at her from the bar. And then again later from the dance floor. Colleen lost track of them and eventually the bartender said, "Last call," and a little later the bar lights came on.

Colleen tried again to get Kevin up. A waitress came over and asked ʻColleen to settle up the rest of the bill. Then Kevin was awake and reaching for the beer in front of him. He downed it before she could stop him. It seemed to wake him up a bit; at least he got to his feet.

She got him outside and looked for Janet. She and Greg were making out over the back hood of his car. She got Kevin pointed in the right direction and pushed him through the small group of people still talking out front. When they got close to the couple, she said, loudly, "We should probably get going."

Janet pushed Greg off her. "Oh, hi." Greg glared, then winked at Colleen.

Colleen opened the back door and let Kevin fall into the seat. She got his legs in, then slammed the door before he could fall out. Greg walked around to the driver's door. Colleen said, "You'd better let me drive, I haven't had anything to drink."

"I'm fine."

"Come on."

"I'm fine. Get in."

"Janet?"

Janet looked drunk herself. But she said, "Colleen's right, maybe you—"

Greg cut her off. "Get in." He slid into the driver's side and started the car.

Colleen shook her head at Janet over the roof.

Greg started to back out and they both stepped out of the way. The car stopped and Greg rolled down the passenger window. "Come on, Janet, let's go."

"I don't want to walk...," Janet said to Colleen.

"He's wasted."

Greg tapped the horn.

Janet got in the passenger side, waving at her sister to follow. Colleen stood and crossed her arms. The car finished backing out and rolled toward the road, where it stopped and idled. Greg stuck his head out the window. "Look, I'm fine. I promise."

Janet leaned over Greg's lap to say, "Come on, Colleen. You're not going to walk all the way home."

Colleen shook her head. Greg shrugged and drove forward a few feet. The car stopped again. Janet got out and said, "Get in. If you don't think Greg is driving good after a mile, we'll pull over and you can drive. Right, Greg?"

Greg held up his hands and smiled out the window.

Colleen hesitated.

Janet said, "Please."

Colleen got in behind Janet. Kevin was passed out on the other side, snoring.

Greg pulled up to the road slowly, then spiked the breaks. Colleen lurched forward.

Janet said, "Grow up," while Colleen said, "Come on."

The wheels of the car started spinning in place and the engine revved. Colleen grabbed the headrest behind Janet while the back end of the car drifted to the left. Then they were going forward, fast.

"Pull over," Colleen said.

Greg stared out the front window at the pool of light in front of the car. The yellow line shuddered by. The car picked up more speed.

"Cut it out, Greg," Janet shouted. A set of headlights appeared ahead of them and flew by.

Colleen knew they were coming up to a tight corner. She said, "You have to slow down, please."

The engine revved into the next gear. Trees appeared at the front edge of the headlights and then Greg slammed the breaks and cranked the wheel. The back end of the car swung out and around. Gravel crunched under them and Kevin flopped across Colleen, pinning her. The car wobbled into a straight line. Colleen pushed Kevin off. "Wake up, make him stop." She hit Kevin's shoulder. He flopped back into the window.

Colleen felt a moment of weightlessness, then slammed into her seat. The bottom of the car scraped the road under her.

Janet grabbed at Greg's arm, telling him to cut it out. Colleen shouted "Asshole," and then they were all bouncing from side to side while the back end fishtailed. Greg wrenched the wheel back and forth, exaggerating each turn. He blew through the stop sign, breaking and sliding them sideways into the intersection. Janet screamed.

"Pull over and let me out," Colleen said. "Now."

They were on a long straight stretch. Greg let the car drift into the oncoming lane. Headlights appeared ahead. Colleen knew Greg saw them. She didn't say anything. She leaned back and closed her eyes. Janet screamed and then the car lurched to the side. The sound of a car horn drew out behind them. Colleen kept her eyes closed and held on to Janet's headrest. She spent a few minutes being jerked from side to side while Janet screamed and swore, but she refused to open her eyes. Then she slammed into the back of Janet's seat.

They were in front of Colleen and Kevin's place.

Colleen opened the door and got out.

Colleen said, "You asshole."

Janet and Greg got out. He said, "Relax, I was just playing."

Colleen walked around to Greg and slapped him. She went for a second slap but he caught it and grabbed her other arm before she could wind up. He said, "I told you, I was just playing. Relax."

"You fucking asshole."

"Come on. I'll give you a hand getting Kevin in."

"Fuck. Off."

Greg pushed her arms and she stumbled back. He opened the side door and Kevin rolled out. Greg gripped him under the arms and started dragging him toward the house. He said, "Get the door."

Colleen didn't move. Janet ran ahead and used her key to open the door. Colleen breathed steadily, collecting her anger.

When Janet and Greg came out, Colleen said, "Let's get in the house."

Greg's face went dark again. He said, "You're coming with me, Janet."

Janet looked at Colleen and then back at Greg. She said, "Come on, it's not a big deal. He said he was just playing."

"He's an ass."

Greg ignored that. He walked over to the car and said, "Let's go."

Janet hesitated.

Colleen said, "Get in the house, Janet."

Janet's sympathy disappeared. She glared at her sister. "You can't tell me what to do."

Greg winked at Colleen over the roof and got in with Janet. She watched them drive away.

The Money

The bathroom door opened into John's foot. He looked up from his phone. Melissa came out in a T-shirt and jeans, and, he noticed, no bra. When she stepped over the futon, John tried to pull her down to the bed. She twisted free and pushed his hand away. "I've got homework," she said.

She grabbed the bra draped over the side of the reading chair and wiggled it on under her shirt. He went back to his phone while she banged around the plastic bins they used for storage. She unwound the hairdryer, stepped over John, and plugged it in.

John read an article on five big hockey trades that might happen. It took him a minute to notice the dryer was off and Melissa was staring at him.

"What?"

"I thought you were going to put up the bed?"

"What's the point?"

"The point is, it takes up half the room when it's down and I feel like we're breathing on each other all the time."

Melissa pulled the pillow out from under his head. John sat up and they wrestled the bed into a couch. There wasn't much more room—just enough to clear a path into the tiled area that served as their kitchen.

"Fuck," she said. "Are you heading out today? I've got homework."

"I could clear out." John got up and pulled on his pants and went into the kitchen. He found a filter, dumped some coffee grounds into it, and then opened the fridge. There was a bottle of ketchup and a balled-up bag of bread. He opened a few drawers and realized Melissa was staring at him again. He said, "Now what?"

"I thought you said you were heading out."

"Now?"

"I need to finish this homework before class."

"Well, I've got to eat."

"Get something from the place around the corner."

"I don't have any money. Lend me a twin?"

"What happened to the twenty I gave you yesterday?"

"I spent it."

"Fuck. I told you my student loan is almost gone. When are you going to hear from your lawyer?"

"End of the month."

"I thought you said it was this week."

"No, I'm seeing the doctor this week."

"Again? God."

Melissa sat down at the table and opened her laptop. She clicked a few times, then looked up at John. "Well?"

"What? I told you, I don't have any money."

"Neither do I, and I'm sick of lending you 'just another twin' so you can give me space in my own house."

"Your house?"

"I pay the rent."

"You know I'm going to pay you back when the money comes in."

"We've been waiting for '*the money to come in*' for over three years."

"You know I hate it when you do that voice."

"'*You know I hate it when you do that voice.*'"

John tried not to take her bait; if he just focused on the fact that their problems were temporary, soon to be resolved by his settlement, things would be fine. But then she brought up all the other things too. She told him he was lazy, even though she knew he couldn't work because of his back. Then she moved on to how he was unappreciative, which, he told her, wasn't true and she knew it. Then she said he needed to contribute money, which she knew he couldn't because he couldn't work and his dad refused to lend him money unless he moved back to their shitty hometown and worked with his old man and that fucking insane asshole uncle of his for the rest of his goddamned life, and that was the one thing she knew he couldn't do because if he worked he would lose the settlement and then he'd be totally fucked, and is that what she wanted? They'd left together to start the new, better life they'd always talked about since they'd first made out in grade six. Did she not believe in that anymore? Did she not love him anymore? He was shouting by the end.

"I do, of course I do," she said and rubbed her sleeve across her eyes. "It's just hard to be so broke and have to do all this studying, and it's hard just seeing you lie around all day and I know it's your back but..." She looked at the laptop screen. "Oh shit. I have to get to school. Fuck, fuck." She slammed the laptop shut and shoved it in her bag, gave her face a wipe and said, "Fuck. This sucks. See you tonight." She ran out of the house.

John lay back down and stretched his back.

. . .

"YOUR DAD SAID TO say hello. And also that there's a job waiting for you if you ever decide to, and I'm quoting him here, 'Get off your lazy good-for-nothing ass and get a job like a real man.'" Chad tapped his full pint glass to the top of John's. "He said some other stuff too, but you can probably guess what it was. You know how your dad gets."

John took a long sip of his beer and stared at his coaster.

"I got to tell you, man"—Chad topped off his glass from the pitcher and did the same to John's—"it's good to get out of that shithole of a town every now and then." He tapped John's glass again. "You must be living the life up here in the city."

"It's not that great."

"No? Laying around the house, fucking Melissa all day, while I'm stuck on some jobsite with your goddamn dad. I got to say, though, he starts to look pretty some days."

"Melissa's not so happy with me."

"Can't get it up?" Chad tapped John's glass with his again.

"We're just pretty broke…"

"Why don't you come home with me? We can tag team your old man together. Solves both your problems: you can get laid and make some cash."

"Fuck. Would you cut that out?"

"Haven't you got that sweet settlement money yet?"

"No..."

"Oh man, what's it been, like four years?"

"Yeah, something like that."

"I can't even believe you're fighting that, man. That was one hundred percent your fault." John looked up and glared, but Chad wasn't looking. He was already laughing. "What the fuck were you thinking? Trying to slam-dunk a fucking basketball at prom? You never even played basketball before. What made you think you could do that? And you made such a big deal, lining it up, getting everyone to watch." Chad laughed. John thought of getting up and heading out, but he knew he needed to take it. Chad kept on: "And then you fucking ran up, jumped up on that chair and *bam*." Chad slapped the top of the table. "You didn't even get near the hoop man. You just fell flat on your fucking back."

"You know I broke my back, right?"

"You're lucky you didn't break your neck. And then the basketball, like, a minute later finally came down and bounced off your face. Oh man, I thought Charlie was going to bust his nut laughing."

"How is Charlie?" Asking about old friends was always a good way to change the subject with Chad. It worked. John got the same update he'd gotten a couple of weeks before, when Chad had come up to the city to blow his paycheque on a night on the town.

John drank his beer and stretched his back. It wasn't the fall he was suing about anyways. He'd told Chad a million times, it was what happened after. The shop teacher who was chaperoning prom had figured John was more drunk than hurt and had given him a lift home. John's dad found him the next morning, still passed out, puking up pink foam. When John came to in the hospital, he was told he had a broken rib, a punctured lung, a concussion, and one cracked vertebra in his back. If his dad hadn't checked on him, there was a good chance he would have died.

Though the fall *was* his fault, the gross negligence of the school and the prom's chaperones, explained the lawyer who had shown up at the hospital, was not. And since the injuries were bound to linger and affect the rest of John's life, the incident could be worth a lot of money.

John's father had been against hiring a lawyer—"If being a drunk moron was a reason to sue, your uncle Rob would be a very rich man," he'd told John. But John's grades weren't going to get him out of town, and the only work experience he had was a summer as a general labourer at his dad's construction company. That was not a career path John was interested in. A big money settlement sounded much better. He hired the lawyer. When his dad found out, he kicked John out of the house. The only choice John had left was to move up to the city with Melissa, who was starting college.

Chad finished the story about Charlie pissing his pants in second grade and waved the waitress over for another pitcher.

"So anyways…" John spun the base of his empty pint around the shredded coaster and looked at the table. "I was wondering if you could spot me a bit of cash."

"Again, man?" Chad laughed. "I drive three hours to visit you on my one day off—the one day of my miserable life I'm not humping hundred-pound blocks across a construction site—and you want to hit me up for my hard-earned money?" He was half smiling, a good sign. He'd just give John a hard time first. "I work, all my life, with your gimp of an uncle and slave-driving father, and all I want to do when I get out is have a beer with my best bud. But then, he hits me up for another fucking loan."

John said, "Ha-ha."

"I wake up this morning alone in a cold apartment. Work all goddamn day in the rain, drive three hours to see my fancy city-boy, who should be living it up, but instead, like a common beggar, he asks me for change."

John said to the coaster, "Look, you know I'm good for it. I'll get you back when I get the money."

"Yeah, I know. You and your fucking money."

JOHN SAID, "I NEED five bucks for the bus."

"Are you fucking kidding me?" Melissa slammed her laptop shut.

"I've got to get to the doctor, remember?"

"Walk."

"My back..."

Melissa stepped over John and went into the bathroom. Eventually, John said to the door, "I need to get going."

There was more silence, and then the door opened into the side of the futon. Melissa stepped by John to her purse and dug around in it. She said, "I don't have any cash."

"Fuck. Lend me your debit."

"Fine, but pick up dinner."

"What do you want?"

"Whatever, I don't care."

"Well, I don't care either."

They argued about what they didn't want for a while before settling on sushi.

John went to the corner store across the street and took forty out of the ATM. The receipt showed Melissa had minus eighty-seven dollars. He bought a pack of smokes and decided to walk to the appointment.

The office of the doctor his lawyer sent him to was in a strip mall in a not-so-great part of town. Five store fronts were lit up with neon signs advertising various services in different languages, and above them were massage places that John was pretty sure were rub-and-tugs. The doctor's office was on the end. Blacked-out windows faced the street, but inside it was all clean and modern. John said hello to the receptionist and took a seat on one of the see-through plastic chairs across from a large, colourful painting of fish. He stared at that for a few minutes, then flipped his way through a golf magazine.

An hour later he was led to an examination room. The doctor came in and asked how he was doing.

John said, "Great."

"I mean your back."

"Oh yeah. Sore."

"Sure, sure." He had John do a couple of stretches, then ran down the same list of questions he asked every time.

"Pain's pretty bad, right?"

"Yeah."

"Still can't do housework?"

"I guess not."

"Looking for a job?"

"No."

"You're feeling down. Can't do anything. Depressed."

"Yeah."

"Great! That's all I need."

The doctor filled out a prescription form and handed it to John. It was for painkillers and antidepressants. John got it filled at the pharmacy on the corner.

He dropped both bottles into the trash on his way home. He didn't need the painkillers—hadn't really since a few months after the accident. When he had started to feel better after moving up to the city, the lawyer had explained that recovery would hurt the settlement. It was important that John still seem to be in constant pain, so the prescriptions needed to be filled. The antidepressants had been the lawyer's idea too; after all, if John was in constant pain as a result of his accident, he was sure to start feeling a bit down.

He got back to the apartment. Melissa asked, "Where's dinner?"

"Oh fuck."

"Seriously?"

"Sorry, it was just packed on the bus and I forgot. Here." He gave her back her debit card.

"You want me to go pick it up?"

"I just got home."

"Without dinner. You know what?" Melissa took a

deep breath and stepped over John to the door. "Never mind. I'm going out."

John waited a couple of hours, reading his phone on the couch, and then went down to the corner store and spent the last of Melissa's change on a bag of chips and a microwaveable burrito.

JOHN WAS ALREADY UP, sitting at the kitchen table, when Melissa came in the next morning. He said, "What happened to you last night?"

"Nothing, I stayed at a friend's."

"What friend."

"Nancy."

"Who's Nancy?"

"From school."

Melissa stepped over a pile of shoes and pivoted into the bathroom. She said through the door, "I've got to get to class."

"You didn't call. Or return my texts."

The shower started. John tried to pace but there was no room. He went into the kitchen area and leaned on the counter.

Melissa came out in a towel and opened the clothes bin and started digging. He said, "I can't believe you just let me sit here."

"Look, I just fell asleep. I didn't mean to stay."

"I was worried."

"Worried you'd have to pay rent?"

"Hey, that's not fair."

"I didn't even have enough left on my card to pay for dinner. How much did you take out?"

"I was going to give you the change, but you left so quick I forgot."

"Okay, well…" She held out her hand.

"I got myself dinner."

"Fuck, that's it. You need to get your own money."

"From where?"

"I don't know, get a job maybe?"

"You know I can't. It would fuck up my settlement."

"I'm sick of hearing about the settlement."

"Well, what do you want me to say?"

"That you're going to get some money, for starters."

"You want me to go home and waste my fucking life working with my dad?"

"There are other jobs. Wait tables or something."

John was about to tell her it would all be okay when he got the money, but she grabbed her bag and left before he could get out the words. He looked at the closed door awhile. They hadn't even really fought; she'd just left. She'd never done that before. He thought about what to do.

If he got a job, the settlement would disappear, and he'd spent too long holding out for it to give up now.

It had been over three years since his lawyer had first told him that not working was going to be key to a big settlement, and he'd taken that advice to heart. Melissa hadn't minded him not working early on; she'd been sympathetic to his pain, didn't complain about always having to cover the rent and buy food. But then they'd got kicked out of the cheap place they shared with three other girls—the roommates had decided that rent should be split five ways by person, rather than four ways by room, which John had convinced Melissa was ridiculous—and suddenly she was putting more of her student loan into rent and things got a lot tougher. She'd had to take summer jobs to make some extra money. Things had gotten rough over the last year. She'd started dropping hints about him getting work and was impatient with him when he claimed back pain. And now, she seemed serious.

There wasn't much else he could do. He'd tapped all of his friends for loans; Chad was the only one who was good for it, but he'd only ever give John a fifty at a time anymore, and only when he came to visit, which wouldn't be for another couple of weeks. There was no way he could call his dad, and that was it for family. He just needed that settlement.

He called his lawyer and left a message with the secretary. Later that day, he called back.

There was no update. No date for a hearing set. "Soon," he said. "You got to be patient."

"I'm broke," John said. "I need to get a job."

"I would strongly recommend not doing that. Our entire settlement ask is based on you not getting to work. If you work..."

"I know, but what am I supposed to do in the meantime? You've been saying soon for years."

"I can't advise you on what to do, but I'd suggest borrowing some money."

"Lend me a few hundred dollars?"

"That would be unethical, and extremely illegal."

"Well, fuck."

"John, listen. We've come this far. You've just got to hold on for a little bit longer."

John hung up. He lay down on the futon and tried to think of a way to buy himself a bit more time.

JOHN TAPPED THE DASHBOARD to the beat of the music until Melissa said, "Cut that out." He did. She moved into the fast lane and passed a few cars.

"Still mad?" he asked. She kept her eyes on the road.

They were on their way home for her reading break. He had wanted to stay behind but he had no money and when he'd asked Melissa for a few bucks, she'd said no way. They got into a fight. He told her there was no way he could go to their town because he hated staying at her parents' house. Her dad made him sleep on the couch and made it clear he didn't like John. And, of course, his dad's house was out of the question. She hadn't budged; in fact, she'd packed his bag with enough clothes to last him for weeks and thrown it in the car, all while telling him he was a complete deadbeat and an anchor on her life. He'd taken offence and they'd yelled at each other on the street, but given the choice between starving or spending some time in his hometown, John caved and eventually got in the car.

Melissa weaved the car in and out of the fast lane, not saying anything. John kept his mouth shut. They had two hours to go. John looked at the passing signs.

Twenty miles later, she said, "Thirty-three thousand, four hundred."

"What?"

"That's how much you owe me. That's half the rent for three years. Maybe a hundred dollars a month for food. Another fifty for bills. Not to mention all the dinners out and all the times you *'Just needed to borrow a twin.'*"

"You know I hate it when you do my voice like that."

"*'You know I hate it when you do my voice like that.'*"

"Come on."

"Well fuck, John. I've spent four student loans on you."

"You know it will all be good when the money comes in."

"Stop saying that. Just. Stop. Saying. That."

They were quiet again. John turned up the radio. She turned it back down. It was an hour to the exit, another half-hour down the long road to their hometown. It seemed longer.

The sign welcomed them. When they turned toward John's house, he said, "I thought we were staying with your folks?"

"I need space."

"Are you fucking kidding me? I can't just drop in on my dad. He'll fucking lose his shit. He told me I wasn't welcome there unless I start working for him. I can't do that, you know I can't—"

She stopped in front of his dad's house. "Get out."

"No."

She turned off the car and pulled the keys from the ignition. She said, "I'll come back for this later."

John followed her. He told her that his dad was psychotic, that he couldn't go home, that she was abandoning him, that it was unfair, and that everything was going to be okay once he got the money and after all they'd been through how could she throw away all their years together. When they got close to her house, he asked her if it was because she was fucking someone else, was that why she was treating him like this? Those nights at Nancy's? Was that what was going on? Was that why she was being such a fucking bitch?

Melissa slammed her parents' door in his face. John saw her dad look out the window and decided to head over to Chad's. He waited on the steps. A few hours later, Chad pulled up in his truck. Said, "Nice to see you bud. What brings you to town?"

"Mind if I crash here?"

"Things going well with Melissa I take it?" Chad tapped John in the crotch, but told him to come on in.

He tried calling Melissa that night and then again the next day. And again the next night. Three days in, he went to her parents' house and knocked on the door. Her dad opened it and said, "She's gone back to the city," and closed the door in his face. Her dad had always been an asshole.

He tried calling her until the end of the week. Finally, she picked up and said, "You have to stop calling, John." It sounded like she was already crying.

"What the fuck is going on?"

"I have to focus on school. It was too hard with you around all the time."

"You're kicking me out?"

She didn't say anything. He screamed into the phone, "Are you breaking up with me? After all these years?" He said a lot of other things too and kept at it until he realized she'd hung up. He put down the phone.

Chad said, "How'd that go?"

JOHN TOSSED HIS TOOLS into the bed of his dad's truck and rubbed his back.

"Oh, does your fucking back hurt, pretty boy?" His uncle Rob threw his tools in beside John's.

"No." He'd been through this before.

Uncle Rob went into it anyways. "I had a fucking wall fall on me. I was pinned under it for six fucking hours before your old man finally realized I was missing and came to find me. Broke three goddamn bones in my back. I still can't feel my left foot. You know how much work I missed?" John did, but Uncle Rob answered before he could respond. "None. I got a back brace and came right back. Pull up your panties and deal with it, you useless fuck."

Chad came out of the trailer with his backpack and a case of beer. He tossed his pack in the truck and passed around beers. He said, "Great pep talk, as always, Bob." He cracked his beer and toasted, "To another fucking week done." They all clinked beers.

Uncle Rob spat and asked for a smoke. He never had his own.

John's dad came out of the trailer. Chad handed him a beer, which he drank while he looked over the site. He found a couple of empty cigarette packages and tossed them in the back of the truck. He said, "Let's head home, boys."

John got in the truck and checked his phone.

Chad said, "Melissa begging for you back?" Chad reached across and slapped John on the penis. "She miss that massive cock of yours?"

"Jesus man. Come on." John tilted his legs to the side and put his beer over his crotch. He tried not to think of her. It had ended poorly — a drive to the city with Chad; Melissa, and the other guy there, "studying," a shouting match, neighbours threatening to call the cops and then back to Chad's and then John called and called and called.

There were no messages on his phone.

They drove from the site to John's dad's house and parked in the back. It was payday, so John's dad went into the house and came out with the beat-up accordion folder he used for accounting. He spread out his papers on the truck's hood, totalled the hours, marked them down in his book, and started to write cheques. Uncle Rob and Chad drank another beer. John went around to the front of the house to check the mailbox.

An official-looking envelope from his lawyer was there. He'd been waiting on it for weeks. It was his settlement cheque, which was "Not worth the fucking time I wasted on this case," according to his lawyer. He'd been furious when John had let him know he'd gone back to work with his dad. The lawyer's whole case had fallen apart and he'd been forced to settle for a much smaller amount than planned. And that amount, John saw now looking over the paperwork, was even smaller after the lawyer's fee and other deductions were taken off. He read everything a second time, then thought about calling his lawyer, but he knew right away that would get him nowhere. The amount was less than the paycheque his dad handed him.

"That from the fucking lawyer of yours?"

John put both cheques in his pocket. He said, "Yeah."

"You didn't get the big payday."

"No."

"I told you, you have to work to earn money."

"I know." He didn't bother arguing that it would have been more if his dad had just loaned him enough money to last a few more months. Or if Chad hadn't said he was too broke to put up John for free. Or if Melissa had just held on a few more weeks.

John's dad softened a bit, as much as he ever did at least. He said, "Look, I'm happy you're working finally. And you know I'm sorry things didn't work out with you and Melissa..." John had a flash of embarrassment — calling, messages, calling again, texting and texting and texting. He forced the thoughts from his mind. His dad went on, "I always liked her. But listen, this is a good job, good money, there's downtime between jobs. Once you get a bit better at things, I can start showing you how to do the books, put together bids. Hell, you can be in business on your own in a few years."

John nodded; it was always the same with his dad.

He went back around the house. Uncle Rob had shaken up a beer and was holding the foam-spraying bottle over his crotch while he chased Chad. He stopped when John appeared. He asked, "You coming to the Oak with us?"

"Sure."

They piled into Uncle Rob's little hatchback for the short drive to the bar. John took out his phone and thought about texting Melissa. He had planned on sending the settlement to her, thought it might be a good excuse to get back in touch with her, to see how things were going. He'd even thought he'd head back to the city, take her out for dinner. Maybe she'd be happy to see him...but it was so little money in the end, not anywhere close to what he owed. By the time they pulled into the bar's parking lot, he'd decided to hold on to what he'd got. There was no reason to pay her back if she wasn't going to talk to him anyways. And he knew then that if he wasn't going to get her back, he had no choice but to stay in town and save up some money and hopefully find a way to get back to the city on his own.

Uncle Rob went straight into the bar while Chad and John finished their beers in the car.

John said, "On me tonight. I got some extra cash."

"Sounds fucking good man, you're only into me for about thirteen hundred more drinks."

They went into the bar and settled in for the night.

When Things Wear Away Other Things

Moira played with the ocean, chasing the waves as they pulled back into themselves. Her pink rain boots splashing through the water were the only colour on the rocky shore. She turned to David and laughed. A wave came in behind her and covered her feet and went over the top of her boots before she noticed. She looked down at the water pulling away and then at her dad, and then did what she always did when she was surprised: she started to cry.

David walked over and picked her up. He told her it was okay, just water, then turned her away from the ocean and asked, "Do you see how they built a wall there?" He held her on his hip in the crook of one arm and pulled her boots off with his free hand. She was trying to tell him about her feet being wet between exaggerated sobs. He said, "Over there. Look. Do you see the wall?"

She didn't say anything, but looked where he was pointing. David continued. "A long time ago, before they built the wall, there was a graveyard here." He dumped the water out of one boot, then the other. "Back then where we're standing was underground." He moved her onto his other hip and tugged off her socks. "But the waves eroded the ground."

She had forgotten that she was supposed to be crying while she tried to follow what he was saying. She asked, "What's 'eroded'?"

David turned back to the water. "See how every time a wave comes up it pulls some rocks back with it? That's eroding. It's when things wear away other things. Eventually, the waves will wear through the wall and wash away the city."

Moira looked at the wall and then the ocean and then her dad. "Really?"

"Yup." He said, "Hold these," and handed her the boots. He pulled off her socks and wrung them out as best he could. "Eroding takes a long time though. Hundreds of years. But anyways, back before the wall was built the waves were eroding the ground, wearing away the graveyard's dirt, and you know what's under the dirt in a graveyard?"

She thought. "Dead people?"

"That's right. And they're in coffins. So when the waves came and wore away the ground, all these coffins were getting uncovered and they started floating out to sea. After bad storms the bay would be full of them, like little boats bobbing around in the water."

"Really?"

"It's true. It was a real problem. And, of course, no one wanted coffins floating around the bay, so they built that wall to keep them in."

David pulled Moira's socks and boots back on and set her down on the ground. She ran up to the wall and looked back at her dad. "*Really?*" He nodded. She ran her hand along the wall. It was pitted and rough, small rocks stuck out where the concrete had worn away around them. She grabbed one of the rocks and pulled. It came off in her hand.

"See," David said. "Just like the coffins."

She held it up close to her face. David looked up the beach and said, "We better catch up with your mother." Katherine had walked ahead while David and Moira dawdled. He could only see her outline against the rocks, but even at that distance, David could feel her impatience.

Moira didn't want to go. She whined and planted herself on the ground and wouldn't budge. David tried unsuccessfully to reason with her and finally he said,

"Bye, have fun," and started walking. When he was thirty feet away, she screamed "Wait!" and ran to catch up. Once she was with him, she climbed up on the driftwood logs piled at the high-tide line and started walking along them, hopping from one to the next. David said, "Could you please try to hurry a bit?"

She said, "I can't put my feet down because of the lava!"

"Come on, please. We don't have time for that."

Moira kept walking on the logs until she got to the end of one that was too far from the next. She stopped and said, "Help!" David went back and bent down in front of her. She climbed onto his back and they picked their way along the rocky shore toward her mother.

Katherine put out her cigarette when they got close. She said to David, "You took your time."

"I didn't realize you had gotten so far ahead."

Moira said, "Dad told me that the ocean took the dead people out to sea because of eroding and all the coffins floated away."

David winced. Katherine said, "Why would you tell her that?"

David put Moira on the ground and crouched down in front of her. He said, "See, I told you it was true." Katherine tilted her head to one side and gave David her are-you-fucking-kidding-me look. He ignored it, instead smiling at Moira, then tickled her and said, "Let's build a sandcastle!"

She looked around the rocky beach and said, "There's no sand."

"Then we'll just have to make do with what we have."

David pulled a piece of driftwood out of a tangle of seaweed and tossed it on the ground. He found another that was roughly the same length and threw it on top. Then another. Moira asked what he was doing and he shrugged and kept pulling out sticks, breaking long ones so they were all the same length. Once he had a pile he carried them down to a flat part of the beach and started driving them into the ground. When Moira saw they were going to make a circle, she said, "It's a wall!"

"You got it. Can you grab me some more wood? Like this." He showed her a stick and she concentrated on it, and then ran over to her mom and grabbed her hand and told her to come help.

David worked on the wall. Moira came back a few minutes later with an armful of all-too-short sticks. She dropped them off and left to find more. Then Katherine came along with her own load. David focused on making sure one stick was in the ground right, but eventually had to turn around and get another. Katherine was staring down at him. He smiled at her. She said, "You think it's funny?"

He shook his head and drove another stick into the ground. "This is ridiculous. You're angry because you walked ahead of us?"

"I'm angry because this was supposed to be a day of us all together and you kept her with you."

"We were having fun and you didn't stop."

"Why are you like this?"

David said, "Almost done" to Moira, who was coming up behind Katherine with more sticks. Katherine walked over to a driftwood log and sat. Moira and David finished the wall, all crooked driftwood leaned together. He planted a few more sticks to fill in the bigger gaps and then stood. He waved his hand over it and said, "Behold, my queen, your ramparts are complete."

Moira looked it over and said, "It needs a roof."

"Absolutely. And a moat. And a drawbridge. It will be the finest sandcastle ever created!"

"It's not made of sand."

"Neither are sandwiches, but we eat them anyways."

"You're silly."

"That seems to be the consensus around here."

"What's 'consensus'?"

"Consensus is when everyone thinks I'm silly."

David started digging a moat with a flat piece of wood. Every scoop out made more pebbles and rocks to fall back in. The best he could manage was a shallow, wide ditch. While he worked, Moira leaned sticks up against the wall, trying to fill in the gaps. Katherine smoked and looked out over the ocean and then Moira got bored with trying to fix the wall and started waving around one of the sticks, commanding David to work faster in a voice that was meant to sound like a queen. David played along, grovelling and shovelling faster. Once the moat was as good as it was going to get, he said, "My queen, I'm going to find a roof."

Up the beach he found some rope tangled up with some driftwood. He pulled it out but there wasn't enough to do anything with. He found some old planks and what looked like a pallet and then a little farther along he found a piece of plywood. He lifted one edge off the ground and gave the crabs time to find new shelter before he started dragging it back. It was waterlogged and heavy and he had trouble getting a good grip.

When he got closer he saw Katherine had left her log. She was crouched on the ground by the castle and Moira was running around picking things up. Moira held something out to Katherine and then they both laughed. By the time David got back to them, they were both sitting on the ground. He said, "A roof for your castle, Your Highness."

Moira said, "Look, we made a garden." They had arranged pieces of shell and wave-worn glass in spiral patterns all around the entrance to the castle. There was a little path too, and small twigs stood upright with seaweed wrapped around the tops. "Those are trees," she explained. "Mom made them."

David said, "That's very clever."

He lifted the plywood over top of the wall and let it down slowly. The castle shifted a bit to the left. Katherine got up and wiped the pebbles off her pants and David found a few large rocks to prop up the side that seemed most likely to give out. He stood back and admired their work. Moira was tending her garden. Katherine tapped her wrist and pointed at the darkening sky.

David said to Moira, "Nothing left to do but move in." He got down on his hands and knees and crawled in. He had to tilt his shoulders, and even still he knocked over one of the wall sticks.

Inside, he tried to shift around and sit without knocking the whole castle over. Moira gave up on the garden and followed him in. David had to pull up his knees under his chin so she had room. He said, "I think it's nicer from the outside."

Moira had just enough space to stand. She said, "I like it."

"I'm not saying it's bad. I just wouldn't want to spend the night here."

"It'd be cold."

"Very."

"We could make it better."

"I don't know, it's getting pretty late."

"Tomorrow?"

"It probably won't be here tomorrow."

"Why?"

"It will be washed away by then."

"Why?"

"It's like the graveyard. It will get eroded by the waves when the tide comes in tonight."

She thought about that. David stretched out one leg as far as the opposite wall and rubbed his lower back. Sand sprinkled down from the ceiling. Through a gap in the wall he saw a freighter passing by on the horizon. The water had darkened to the same colour as the clouds. It looked like it was cutting through the air. Moira asked, "Can we stop it?"

David took a moment to realize she was talking about the erosion, not the freighter. "I don't think so. We'd need to reinforce it with something. Concrete maybe. Do you have any concrete?" She shook her head. "Then I think we're out of luck."

Moira sat down across from her dad. Their knees touched. Now that they weren't moving, David started to feel the cold and wet of the day.

Outside, Katherine said, "It's getting cold. We should get going." Moira said no and Katherine said, "I don't want you to catch a cold." Moira said no again and David didn't say anything. Katherine stared at the castle. She said, "Five minutes," then sat back down and lit another cigarette.

Moira smiled at the extra time and turned to her dad, practically face to face. She said, "Would magic save the castle?"

"Well, of course. Magic saves anything. You didn't say you had any magic."

Moira picked up a stick. "This is a wand!"

"What luck! Do you know a protection spell?"

Moira waved the wand over her head while chanting something close to words. She touched the stick to the wall and spun around the whole castle. Then she tapped David's nose with it. "You're protected too."

"That's great."

She waved the wand out the door, then looked around the castle, suddenly bored. David pulled her down onto his lap. He rubbed her shoulders. She banged her wand on the ground between their legs and stuck the stick in the sand, then swirled it around to make a hole.

Eventually, Katherine said, "Time to go."

Moira looked back at her dad. David kissed the top of her head and then wrapped his arms around her. He said, "We can wait a few more minutes." They listened to the waves dragging the beach into the sea.

What She'd Remember

Nick sat out the side of his truck with his elbows on his knees and his head hanging down between them. The morning zoo crew talked at him from the radio. Randy stood behind his truck, pulling his tools out of the back. He slammed the tailgate shut.

Nick said, "Fuck."

Randy walked around front and grabbed his Thermos out of the cab. He held it out to Nick. Nick looked up, then reached under his seat and pulled out a cup. He wiped it with an old rag. Randy filled Nick's cup and asked, "Aren't you a little old for all these late nights?"

Nick shook his head in a way that meant yes. They drank their coffees and listened to the hits until the DJ came on and gave the time. Randy turned off the radio and said, "Pitter patter."

Nick said, "Fuck off with that shit," but flicked
the last drops of his coffee at the ground and tossed
the cup back in the truck. Nick tied up his boots,
clipped on his Kuny sack, and limped after Randy
toward the jobsite.

Randy lifted a couple pallets of blocks up to the
top of the scaffolding with the forklift while Nick got
the mixer going. He hiked his jogging pants over his
belly and dumped a bag of cement in the mixer, then
added the water. When it was mixed, he dumped the
mud into a wheelbarrow and pushed that onto a pallet
that Randy had lifted up top. Then they climbed up,
Nick slowly, taking one rung at a time. The sun was
just coming up over the trees.

Four buildings were going up on the site. The first
was done and the tenants, a brake and lube place, had
already moved in. The second building was just getting
its roof. Randy and Nick had done the block work on
the first two and would be done the third building in
a few more weeks. Then they'd start on the fourth,
which was just a hole in the ground waiting for the
foundation to be laid. When the job was done, four
identical cinder-block warehouses would stand in a
row along the highway. It was shit work to put up ugly
buildings, but at least it was steady for a few months.

The other trades showed up while Nick and Randy
worked. Some of the guys shouted hellos up to them.

One had been out the night before; he let Nick know he'd lost a bet about whether or not Nick would make it in to work. Nick flipped him the bird.

When the sun rose high over the buildings, Randy took off his sweater and Nick sat on a pallet and stripped down to his faded fluorescent swimming trunks.

Nick said, "Anyways, I got to head out at lunchtime today."

"What for?"

"Doctor."

"Again? You okay?"

"Never have been."

"I'm serious, you good?"

"Can't imagine it's too good when they call you back in."

"Well shit. Let me know if you need anything."

"I'll be fine. Let's get back to it."

Nick scooped mud onto his trowel and slid it along the edge of the blocks, covering about four feet's worth of wall. He grabbed a block with his good arm and pulled it onto his hip and gave himself a few seconds' rest before hauling it over the top of the rebar and lowering it into place. He tapped the block straight with the butt of his trowel, and then did the same with another. Before the mud dried, he and Randy double-checked with the plumb line and level to make sure it was all square, then Nick ran the jointer between the blocks to clean up the mud that had squished out. They did this over and over, the wall slowly getting taller.

At ten the food wagon came by. They climbed down and Nick bought a doughnut and drank two more cups of coffee while the crew all shot the shit. Most of the guys sat down on their lunch coolers; Nick ate standing up, legs apart and leaning over a skid of bricks to avoid sitting on his hemorrhoids.

They worked through the morning. Just before noon, the building a couple of feet taller, Nick pulled his jogging pants back on and said to Randy, "I'll see you Monday."

Randy said, "Take care, okay?"

"HOW LONG HAVE I been your doctor?"

"I guess we started coming to you when Alice was pregnant with Jake. Maybe thirty years?"

"That sounds about right. And what have I been telling you all that time?"

"Usually to stop smoking."

"And drinking. And eating whatever it is you eat that makes your cholesterol tests look like they got dropped in a deep fryer."

"That's funny."

"I try to keep things light. Anyways, we both know you've never listened to me and now I have to tell you that it's time to stop."

"Yeah, I'll cut back."

"No. That's not going to cut it this time. If I were a betting man, I'd say the cirrhosis is going to be the one that kills you, but the over-under on a heart attack is close."

"Jesus. Do you talk to everyone like this?"

"You're a big boy. Do you want to look at the reports?" The doctor held out a clipboard; Nick shook his head. "I'll break it down for you. Six months, a year at the outside."

"Fuck."

"If you cut everything out, the drinking, the smoking, you might get a few more years."

"Fuck."

The doctor sat down, softened. "Look, Jake was in here with your granddaughter the other day. Cute girl."

"Yeah. Don't know where she gets that from."

"You clean up a bit, maybe you'll live long enough that she remembers you."

"Jesus."

"Up to you though."

They sat there a minute. Nick said, "That it?"

"I could give you the numbers of some alcohol treatment places."

Nick waved his hand. The doctor nodded. "Yeah, I figured."

"I guess I'll be seeing you."

"I hope so, Nick."

A CASE SLID DOWN to replace the one Nick pulled out of the cooler. He closed the door and limped over to the checkout where the clerk said, "You been keeping out of trouble, Nickie?"

"You know it. Give me a pack of Player's too."

Nick pulled a roll of twenties from his pocket and handed two over. He waved off the change. The clerk said, "What's this for?"

"Have a few on me after you get off work."

"I can't..."

"Sure you can. You always been good to me."

Nick dropped the case on the floor in front of the passenger seat and took out a beer. He lit a cigarette and pulled out of the parking lot, keeping the bottle out of sight between his knees.

He'd normally go home and have a couple of drinks before heading out for dinner and a night at the pub, but he didn't want to be in his cramped little bachelor apartment right then. Instead, he drove through town and up hospital hill to where the roads curved around old properties that weren't quite close enough to each other to make it a subdivision. He'd lived out that way a long time ago, when he first moved to town.

This was the first part of town that expanded back in the seventies, during the start of the boom. Back when people still wanted trees between them and their neighbours and it seemed like there was enough space for everyone. Nick drove by the first piece of land he'd bought when he moved out here. The contractor he'd worked for then had given him a no-interest loan to get the lot, and the whole crew had pitched in to put up the house; he'd done the same for them when they got their own land, all of them working with each other during the week and for each other on weekends. It was exhausting, but they were young then and could always find the energy to help each other out.

He was surprised to see the house he'd built was torn down, and a new one, too big for the lot, in its place. That made no sense: a well-built house, only thirty-five years old, shouldn't be torn down. He'd only lived in the house a year, sold it for a good profit, then bought another piece of property—but it was the principle. So much wasted effort.

Randy's first place was still up, a few doors down. They'd done the brickwork on that house together. It had been good back then. Everyone helped each other with the hard work and then they'd all raise hell together when they were done. He'd gotten married and had Jake. The marriage didn't last, but most of the others' didn't either; there were years when everyone seemed to be taking turns sleeping on each other's couches. But he had money to burn—bricklayers were the best-paid trade back then. Now, even drywallers made better money.

He drove around the roads that crossed each other and dead-ended with no rhyme or reason. There hadn't been city-planning back then—a developer just bought a parcel of land and cut it up into lots; the roads were built around the features of the land, not cut in straight lines. He ended up outside the house he'd settled in the longest—still there. He was happy to see it looked the same. It was another one he'd built himself, a split-level, half-brick place.

Most of his family memories were here. They'd moved in when Jake was ten, and Nick had moved out just before the boy turned sixteen. Jake's mom had held on to it until he finished school, then sold it. Nick had never owned a house after that one, just rented apartments. Jake seemed no worse for the divorce; he was a smart kid who worked for the municipality now, made good money. His wife commuted up to the city, worked at some law firm. And their daughter, Nick's granddaughter, Lily, was a beautiful little kid. She'd be coming up on six, starting school soon. Or had started. Nick couldn't remember. He didn't see her as much as he would have liked; the wife didn't care for him.

He looked over his old brickwork from the road, making sure it was still in good shape. It was.

Nick drove to the far end of town on the old highway and turned off onto one of the logging roads. Less chance of running into a roadblock there. The town was getting so you couldn't do anything. There hadn't even been cabs to take you home after the bar until a decade ago. The road took him over an old wooden bridge and up the side of a mountain. He stopped at a small lake he knew in one of the valleys. He finished his beer and listened to the radio and thought it was only a matter of time before the area was all houses.

A Jeep full of kids came out of the woods on the other side of the water, close enough that Nick could hear their music over his. They all got out and one of them saw him looking and said something to his buddies. They laughed and then another one said, "Hey man, you want a toke?" They all laughed again. Nick toasted them with his beer and headed out.

The logging roads took him over the other side of the mountain and then suddenly he was on paved roads that were new since the last time he'd been through. He'd heard they'd subdivided this area.

There were lots marked out with neon flags and *For Sale* signs, a few sites cleared of trees. The houses would all be up against each other, no real yards, just a strip of lawn between. That was no way to live. And it was expensive; all the money went into the mountain view, so the developers went cheap on materials. The houses would all be vinyl-sided or stuccoed. They wouldn't last twenty years before they'd need to be redone. Brick was better—it lasted longer—but it was more expensive, so none of the developers wanted to use it. Better to build a house on the cheap and let the buyer deal with the repairs down the line.

Nick drove around the new streets until he came to a lookout point—a little grassy area and a couple of park benches with a view of the valley. He parked and sat at one of the picnic tables. Lit a cigarette and sipped his beer. He saw how much the town had grown, built out instead of up. The whole valley had filled up with buildings and he'd had a hand in building most of them. He thought it was a nice view; he should come up here more often.

A couple walked by with their dog and gave his truck a dirty look and then him a worse one. A minute later another couple came by; they had a dog too. They let him know he shouldn't be drinking. He told them it was non-alcoholic. They didn't believe him, or take him up on the offer of a beer. He cleared out.

He headed away from town, out to the bay. His son lived out that way and he thought he'd maybe pop in. It was early enough that Jack's wife would probably still be on her way home from the city. It would just be his son and granddaughter; he could get a bit of quality time in. Nick pulled into their subdivision. It had always bothered him that they'd moved here. He'd offered to help them pick out a lot and build them a proper place, but they'd wanted something finished, ready to move into.

Both Jack's car and his wife's were in the driveway; Nick drove by without stopping. He'd have to give them a call later, set something up for the next day. The wife always insisted on having notice, even though it seemed no matter how much notice he gave, they always had plans. Nick drove through the subdivision and back onto the main road.

He took the long way back, around the lake and past the old farmhouses. The owners of one property he passed had him build a brick wall along the road a few years before. It looked ridiculous—too low to keep anything out, and he'd always thought it would be a pain to get out of the car and open the gate they'd had him put in. But they paid well and in cash, so he didn't complain. And it beat the industrial jobs he'd been getting the last few years. There'd been no work but warehouses and garages, cinder-block shoeboxes, nothing to them but putting one block on top of another. And even that was beginning to slow down. He was lucky to get a half-dozen jobs a year and they were nothing he was proud of. Not like the old all-brick houses, or the fireplaces he'd built years before—open-front stonework that took up a whole wall, with tiled stone all around. He'd have to find how to fit each irregular stone with another, like putting together a jigsaw puzzle. It took time and skill. But no one wanted fireplaces anymore. Just like no one wanted brick houses either. Just cinder-block warehouses.

But work was work and those warehouses were a thing he could say he'd had a hand in, and a thing that would last long after he was gone. He didn't dwell on that line of thinking; he wasn't ready for it yet.

There was a roadblock just before the highway. Nick threw his jacket back over the case and stashed his open beer between the seats. The line inched forward, one car at a time. Nick recognized the cop that came over to his window; it was one of the old guys.

The cop shook his head when he saw Nick. "Hey Nick, how many you had?"

"Just three."

"You sure?"

Nick pulled his jacket off the case and tilted it to show how many were missing.

"That probably puts you over, you know?"

"I figured I'd better tell the truth, or you'd give me a hard time for lying. Besides, you wouldn't have believed me if I said none."

"You're right, I wouldn't." The cop looked down at Nick, weighing his options.

Nick said, "You know I wouldn't be driving if I'd had too many."

"I don't want to hear that. Listen, I'm off work in an hour. If your truck is not parked outside of your apartment when I drive by, I'm going to make things hard on you, okay?"

"Sure. Thank you."

"Don't thank me. And for fuck's sake, don't hit anyone on your way home."

Nick went straight through town to his apartment block. He parked close to the road and went up to his room. He had a beer while he showered and a cigarette in front of the TV. *Jeopardy* was on. He guessed a few answers and when he didn't get any right, he turned it off. He pulled on a pair of jeans and a clean button-down shirt and walked down to the bar.

"IS LILY UP?"

"Dad? It's the middle of the night, no one is up."

"I was thinking we could go for a drive tomorrow."

"Dad, can't this wait?" Then, muffled, "It's my dad."

"Yeah, I was just thinking it'd be nice to see her, maybe show her a few things I built around town."

"You been drinking?"

"Only a bit."

"You shouldn't call here when you're drunk, I've told you that."

"It won't happen again."

". . ."

"So, how about a drive tomorrow? I'll pick you guys up around eleven."

"You going to be up by then? It's pretty late."

"I'll be up."

"Why don't you call when you get up?"

"I'll be there, don't worry."

"Sure, Dad, sounds good. Can I get some sleep now?"

"Yeah, sorry to call. I just thought it'd be nice to show her some things, so she'll know I built them."

"Get some rest, Dad."

"Tomorrow?"

"Yeah, Dad, tomorrow."

Nick hung up the phone and felt around the coffee table for his cigarettes. The pack was empty. He picked up a couple of bottles and drank the ends of them. Then he lay back on the couch and wondered what his granddaughter would remember about him.

Unpacking

"It's been six months since Mom died," Anne said. "You really should make the place your own."

Margaret knew that. "I know, I know," she said as she put her coffee down on the kitchen table so she could rub her eyes.

"You haven't changed *anything* since you moved in."

"I know, I know. It's just, how would you feel getting rid of all Mom's stuff?"

"I'd feel fine about it. You know Mom. She just had things because she needed things to decorate with—it's not like she really cared about any of this." Margaret went over to the wicker knick-knack shelf and picked up a miniature of two frogs kissing with a heart between them. "I mean, she left you the condo so you could move out of that tiny apartment. Not to preserve crap like this."

Margaret said, "I know, I know."

She excused herself to the bathroom and ran the water. She stared into the mirror. In the reflection, she saw the picture of two kittens playing in a pile of yarn that her daughter had insisted the family buy her grandma as a housewarming present when she'd moved into the condo ten years before. Her mom had it framed, and with nowhere else for it to go, politely hung it in the guest bathroom. The paper had warped and discoloured from the steam of the shower. Margaret turned off the water and went back out to the living room.

Anne said, "You can start small. Look at this stuff." She gestured at a bookshelf. "There's nothing here that had any meaning for Mom."

"But those are her books."

"Did you ever know Mom to read anything other than *Reader's Digest*? These are just for show." Anne pulled a book from the shelf and read, "The Classics Library, *Don Quixote*. Do you really think Mom read this? I mean, she ordered half of these off TV."

Anne sat down in her mom's over-puffy armchair and looked at the spines. They were all matched sets, arranged by height. One series was on mysteries of the ancient world. Another was about the mysteries of the Far East. Another was mysteries of space. She remembered the commercials that had aired back in the eighties. "I guess so . . ."

"Great. Let's get some boxes."

Anne brought Margaret down to the underground parkade and together they got two armloads of flattened cardboard boxes out of the recycling bin. Back in the condo, they rebuilt them and taped the bottoms. Anne pulled all the books off the shelf and loaded up the boxes.

She said, "Isn't that better?"

Without the weight of the books, the shelf had shifted slightly to the left. Margaret said, "Not really . . ."

"Where are your books?"

"In Mom's room."

"Let's take them out." Anne pushed herself up and dusted off her knees and went into her mom's old bedroom. She said, "Oh, Margaret . . ."

The room obviously wasn't used. It smelled stale, like her mother's perfume under a layer of heavy must. Margaret had put the room back in order the day after she found her mom — putting clean sheets on the bed and vacuuming the trail left by the gurney wheels — and had only come in twice since. The first time to grab the jewellery box so Anne could pick out a few keepsakes, the second time to move in her boxes. They were stacked against the wall.

Anne said, "This seems a bit weird. You're going to leave it like this forever?"

"I wasn't comfortable moving in here. I sleep on the couch..."

Anne left and came back with an armload of boxes. She said, "Let's get this cleaned up."

Anne went into the ensuite bathroom. Margaret heard clattering and followed her in. Her sister was pulling things out of the medicine cabinet and dumping them into a box. The sources of the lingering smells — her mom's hand creams, face creams, foot creams. All her little tonics to battle age. The strongest fragrance was her mom's perfume. The scent had been discontinued years before; Margaret and Anne had gone in on buying her a dozen bottles so she would always have some. As Anne dropped a half-used bottle into a box, Margaret realized it had been a lifetime supply.

"You don't need to cry," Anne said. "You can't hold on to Mom's toothpaste forever." Anne tossed out an old toothbrush, then stopped. "I'm sorry."

"No. It's the perfume. Mom loved it so much."

"Oh, yeah. The only scent she'd wear." Anne opened the counter under the sink. "Here." She handed Margaret an unopened bottle. "We don't have to throw out everything. Keep the stuff that has a memory, get rid of the rest." She pulled out five more full bottles and dropped them into the box. "But you don't need them all."

It took two boxes and five minutes for Anne to finish emptying the bathroom. Anne dropped the boxes in the hall and said, "All right, let's do the bedroom."

Margaret stood in the doorway. There were drawers full of her mom's clothes, a closet full of coats. On the wall there was a painting a teenaged Anne had done; it had hung in every house her mother ever owned. Beside it, a decorative plate that said *Mexico* on it and some hand-painted masks, probably from the same trip. And a photo of her dad, standing in front of their old house, looking like he was in the middle of saying, "Have you taken it yet?" Margaret felt tears coming on.

Anne said, "Maybe I should get started in here. You work on the living room."

Margaret agreed.

She sat in her mom's chair and took stock of the room. Maybe the chair would have to go, but that could wait until she found something better. The couches were all good, and the side tables. She liked the lamps too; her dad had made them out of wood-stained popsicle sticks. They looked like fire watchtowers. Margaret wanted to hold on to those.

The TV cabinet had a shelf of VHS tapes; those

could probably go. They were all classics — *Gone with the Wind*, *The Wizard of Oz*, Fred Astaire musicals. Now that she thought about it, they'd all been bought by her, as presents, for her mom.

She stacked the tapes neatly in a box and moved down to the next shelf. A collection of miniatures from the trip Anne and her family had taken to Disneyland: the Cheshire cat, an Alice with both arms broken off, the Mad Hatter. Anne was right: they were just decoration, with no real attachment to her mom. They could go. Margaret went into the kitchen and pulled some newspaper out of the recycling bin. She wrapped each piece carefully and put them all in a box to be donated. She looked into the box and thought she'd made a good start.

Anne said from the hall, "I'm done." There were stacks of boxes behind her. She came into the living room and looked at Margaret's two half-packed boxes. "That's it?"

"It's just . . . it's hard."

"Come on. None of this stuff is Mom. None of this stuff is our memories. Mom wasn't sentimental about things. Remember how she threw out all Dad's stuff the week after he died?"

"That was awful."

"It did seem a bit quick. But she knew she had to move on. And she'd want you to, too."

"It's just, it's her stuff."

Anne went over to the wall and said, "This is a shellacked puzzle of the Kremlin. Do you really want to keep it?"

"Not really," Margaret said. "But Mom made it, and she hung it up. She must have liked something about it, you know? It's a little piece of her."

"I never once heard Mom mention Russia. She just needed to hang things up, so she used what she had." Anne took it off the wall and put it in a box. It curved, cracking along the middle. "Trust me, she wouldn't want you to hold on to this."

Anne went through the living room, pulling things off the wall, clearing shelves of knick-knacks. Then she did the same in the dining room. She slowed down when she hit the china cabinet full of family photos — the grandkids in sports uniforms, at graduation, staged family shots. Anne looked them over then said, "We have copies of these," and started clearing them out.

They found twenty photo albums in the drawers under the cabinet. Anne said, "Oh boy," and piled them on the dining room table. Anne flipped through one, Margaret another. Anne dropped hers into a box.

Margaret said, "Shouldn't we keep these?

"What's the point?" She was flipping through another. "Do you need three hundred photos Dad took of this rock in Ireland?"

"That's the Blarney stone! Dad's great-grandpa grew up near it."

"Well, if you forget what it looks like you can google it." Anne dropped the album into a box. "We don't even know who these people are." It was true. After retirement, their parents had taken to going on group vacation tours. Their dad had bought his first camera then. The photos were all of strangers, poorly framed scenery shots, or their mom standing in front of buildings looking like she was either about to smile or had just finished. Almost all the albums were from the last decade of her dad's life. The photos from before had already been divided up, and there were no photos from after; their mom hadn't cared for photography.

Anne dropped the last of the albums into a box, then ducked down to pull out something. She said, "Look at this." It was an old black-and-white photograph of their parents. They were in a fake jail, gripping the bars. A wax-work police officer stood beside them. Her mom was smiling, having a great time. Anne said, "Dad looks like he's asking if the picture's been taken yet."

Margaret laughed. "He was always so impatient with people."

"That's probably where I get it from." Anne laughed and then looked down at the photo for a long time. She said, "Can you scan a copy for me?" and wiped her eyes.

"Of course."

Anne said, "I know I'm pushy, but this is for the best. You can't live your life with Mom's stuff all around you."

Margaret said, "I know, I know. Thank you."

The sisters hugged across the table and then Anne took a look around the room. She said they'd made a pretty good start, but it was getting late and she should be heading home. At the door, Anne said she'd send her son by to pick up the boxes for Goodwill and the dump. They hugged again and then Margaret was alone in her bare condo.

She went back into the kitchen and looked at the photo of her parents. They looked so young, so happy. She smiled and put the photo in the middle of the china cabinet, and then went into her mom's room to start unpacking her own things.

Stewart and Rose

It was touch and go for a bit, but Stewart got through the worst of the pneumonia and the doctors were confident he'd make a full recovery. His sons took turns driving down from the city to visit him in the hospital. He told them he could never understand why they bothered to keep old guys like him dying for so long—it was a drain on the system. They tried to cheer him up, but on every visit he was the same. He only wanted to talk about how to divide his money, and how, if he went under again, he didn't want to be revived. After about thirty minutes of this talk, the son would say he had to be getting back to the city, give his dad a pat on the shoulder, and head out.

Outside the room, Rose would be waiting, working on her crossword. They'd ask her how their dad was *really* doing, and she'd say, "He's fine. Just likes to put on a show," and they'd both chuckle. Then she'd add something like, "You know I'm very fond of your father, but he can be a bit of a baby when it comes to getting old."

Then Rose would go back in and pull her chair up beside Stewart. She'd flip through the channels until she found the news, and then ask him if he wanted anything. "Just to get out of this place. But the way things are going, the only way that'll happen is in a casket."

And Rose would always say, "If you talk like that, I'm going to leave."

Then she'd read him crossword clues and he'd doze off. At seven she'd flip over to *Wheel of Fortune*. She'd always get the answers before him, but he was better at *Jeopardy*. At eight, the nurse would come in and apologize for visiting hours being over. Rose would say she had to go and Stewart would say, "I'll be lucky to make it through the night."

"And you'll be lucky if I bother coming in again with you talking like that." Then she'd kiss Stewart goodnight and head home.

ROSE AND STEWART HAD known each other most of their lives. Stewart and his wife Margaret had children the same age as Rose and Jim's. The couples had met each other at a parent-teacher night when their first kids were in kindergarten, and would always say hello and catch up on gossip at school events after that. Twice a year Margaret would bring her kids into the shoe store Rose managed and Rose would marvel at their growth and fit them with new shoes. Any time one of Rose and Jim's kids got hurt, they'd end up being treated by Margaret, a nurse at the local hospital. They were friends in the sense that they knew and liked each other, but their lives were busy enough that things never went much further than that.

After the last of their children were out of school, the two couples saw less of each other. Just chance encounters at the grocery store or around town. One night, they were all at the same restaurant and Stewart insisted that Rose and Jim join him and Margaret. They had a wonderful night and all agreed they should certainly do it again. Anytime they ran into each other after that, they'd remind each other of what a good time they'd had and make plans that never came to anything.

Stewart was the first to retire. Rose read about it in a joke announcement some guys at the mill put in the paper. She said to Jim, "Now isn't that cute, 'After years of being retired on the job, Stewart Berger has made it official.' We should send them something." Jim didn't want to; he said if they wanted a present, they should have sent an invitation. Rose sent a card with both their names at the bottom anyways.

Jim retired a couple of years later and talked Rose into doing the same. "Life is too short," he said. "We should try to have some fun while we still have our health." They booked a cruise to celebrate and the first night on the boat, they bumped into Stewart and Margaret in line for the buffet. They marvelled over the size of the world and joined each other for dinner. They made plans to meet at the pool the next day. That turned into lunch and then an excursion into port and by the end of the cruise neither couple could believe they'd waited so long to be the friends they'd always thought they were.

Back in town, they started meeting at the Denny's every week, and the ladies took to running errands together and talking on the phone every few days. Once a month they'd go to the city for dinner at a nice restaurant. They had a lifetime of stories to share with each other, swapping different perspectives on decades-old gossip. The friendship was mostly driven by the two women—the men couldn't agree on much other than how lazy the new generation was—but they had a good time together regardless. They booked a cruise together again, a year after the first, and then it became an annual tradition.

• • •

MARGARET GOT CANCER FOR the first time at age seventy. Rose helped out by driving her to appointments and, when Margaret was at her worst, brought over meals frozen in Tupperware. A small woman to start, Margaret shrunk to almost nothing during her treatment. They tried to keep her spirits up, even taking her to the Denny's one night, but she was miserable there and couldn't eat, and when it was time to leave, she was too weak to move. Jim and Stewart had to carry her between them to the car. After that she refused to leave the house for anything but medical appointments.

The cancer stabilized for a few months, but then came back stronger than ever. Her hair was gone by then, and she was frail and skeletal; she didn't want anyone to see her like that and asked Rose to stop coming by. They still spoke on the phone every day. Margaret told her she was taking more treatment, even though the doctor said it might not do much good. "I'm not just going to lie back and die," she told Rose. "If there's any sort of chance, I'll take it." She never did give up, and dying took her a long time.

At the funeral, Rose and Jim waited in the line of well-wishers. By the time they got to Stewart, he was slumped down, his normally tall frame lost in a suit that looked three sizes too big. Jim shook his hand and told him what a strong woman Margaret had been.

Stewart nodded and stared at the floor for a long time and then said, "That's what they all say"—he gestured at the crowd of neighbours and family—"that she was strong." He looked like he was done and Jim moved to shake his hand again, but Stewart said, "She wasn't, you know. Not really. She wasn't fighting to stay alive; she was fighting to *not* die. It terrified her. Dying."

Rose broke the awkward silence that followed by giving Stewart a hug goodbye and saying she'd be in touch. On the drive home, she said it felt like there were only bones inside his suit. She wondered if it was the stress, or if he had something too. They both doubted he would last long without Margaret.

Rose called Stewart every week to check in. She carried the conversation, and when Stewart did get going, he only talked about loneliness and death. She was sympathetic for a few months, but then she told him he had to snap out of it; Margaret wouldn't have wanted him just sitting around the house feeling sorry for himself. She tried to get him to come out for dinner with her and Jim. Stewart always said he appreciated the thought but that he just wasn't ready. There would be a long silence where Rose felt like she should try harder before Stewart would say he had to be going. Then she would tell Jim about the talk and try to convince him to give Stewart a call, but he always said that a man has to find his own way out of sorrow, that there was nothing he could do about it. Rose would say something about men and feelings and that would be the end of it.

But still, Rose felt she owed it to the memory of her friendship with Margaret to keep up the calls, even as they became a chore. When she finally did forget one day, she decided to put it off for a full week. After that, her calls became infrequent, eventually settling into a nagging feeling in the back of her head that she really should check in with Stewart.

JIM'S CANCER WAS QUICKER than Margaret's. He went in to see the doctor after a few days of stomach pain, had some imaging done, and was in surgery within two weeks. After he came out of the anaes- thetic, the doctors told him and Rose that the cancer was more widespread than they had thought. He had three months; treatment might help, but would likely only buy him a month or two. Jim got the family together and explained that if it was a matter of three months of dying versus four of pain, weakness, and dying, he'd rather get it out of the way. He didn't want to linger like Margaret. He died three months to the day after the surgery.

The funeral was small and mostly family. At the reception Rose met with the few well-wishers and

thanked them all very much for coming, and then
Stewart was standing there in front of her in the
same too-large suit he'd worn to Margaret's funeral,
looking just as frail. He shrugged nervously and Rose
said she was sorry that she hadn't called in so long,
and he said no, he understood, and was sorry for what
happened. He shook her hand and said he'd like to
stop by once things calmed down, if he could. She
said, of course.

Stewart showed up with flowers a few weeks later.
They talked about their old dinners, their outings
together, the cruises. They played three hands of crib
and then she offered him dinner, which she reheated
from the meals she froze at the start of the week. They
ate on trays while watching the news. Neither talked
about their spouses.

They saw each other a couple of times a week
after that. Always at Rose's, and Jim always brought
flowers or chocolates. He seemed to recover some of
his vitality; his stoop disappeared, he put on some
weight. She enjoyed the visits—they kept her from
dwelling too much on the empty house—but she was
worried Stewart might be getting the wrong idea.
She told him after dinner one night that it was far
too soon after Jim's death for anything more than
friendship. He cut her off and said he understood, and
for now he was just happy to have someone to spend

time with. A friend. He told her that he'd let himself get too depressed after Margaret died. Seeing Jim's obituary had snapped him out of that and given him something to do — to make sure an old friend didn't fall into the same funk.

They grew closer, despite her misgivings. They spent all their days together and, eventually, started to kiss each other hello and goodnight. Even as they grew closer, she never let him spend the night, always insisting he head out at nine. He'd get in his old Cadillac and drive across town to his home, only to come back the next morning with something sweet to go with their morning coffee. A few months passed like that and then Rose brought him to a family dinner and introduced him as her "gentleman caller," a term her children found adorable enough to lessen their surprise over the fact that she seemed to have moved on from their dad.

A year after Jim died, Stewart asked Rose to marry him. She said no; she liked him but she had always thought she'd be married just the one time. He was a bit indignant and didn't come around for a few days, but eventually he got over it. He tried again a month later, this time with an argument ready: "For a year I didn't see a point in living. Now I have a reason to get up in the morning; without you, I'd die." She said that was very sweet, but maybe a little dramatic. She assured him he had her, but suggested he stop it with the death talk.

He tried again a few months later, after a cold had kept him in bed a few days. He told her he was sure he was going to die soon—it was just a matter of time—and it would mean a lot to him if she would marry him. She said it was ridiculous to think a cold was a reason for them to get married, and that she was frankly getting tired of him talking about death all the time. She wanted to enjoy the time they had left, not spend it with a man who was going to spend his last days talking about it being his last days. She left in a huff and he called her to apologize and they spent a long time making up. It ended with her accepting a ring, but she refused to say they were engaged. It was, she said, just to show that she was spoken for.

"WHAT WILL YOU DO without me?" Stewart asked.

"Don't be silly. The doctors said you'll be home by the end of the week."

"But it will only get worse."

"Stewart, really. You've been saying that as long as we've been together. What's a four-letter word for 'God of War'?"

"Those damn kids of mine have abandoned me here."

"They visit every day."

"Out of obligation. Their wives never come, I never see the grandkids."

"Because they'll see you this weekend, *when you're home.*"

"I could be gone by then."

Rose rolled her eyes and wrote in *Hera*. Then she said, "Starts with *A*, four letters, fast planes." A little later, she muttered, "Well, that can't be right." Stewart had closed his eyes and dozed off. A few minutes later Rose stood up. Her leg got tangled in the lines of the IV, and when she turned to get free, she lost her balance and fell over the chair. She screamed and Stewart sat up and tried to stand. She said, "No, don't. Just call the nurse."

Rose had broken her leg and wrist in the fall. "Frail old bones," she told Stewart over the phone. "My own damn fault for being so clumsy." She was laid up in bed at home and would be for weeks. Her daughter Linda had moved in to help out, and had set up a baby monitor so she could call if she needed anything. "Can you believe that? A baby monitor. There's no dignity in getting old."

Stewart couldn't wait to get out of the hospital and take care of Rose. He thought maybe he could move in while she recovered so Linda could get back to her family. Rose didn't promise anything, but did agree that would be convenient and, she added after Stewart huffed, pleasant.

ROSE DIED A FEW nights before Stewart was due to check out. A blood clot had formed in her broken leg and moved to her heart. Stewart got the news from Linda the next morning. She sat with him until his son showed up, then excused herself to get back to her family. His son asked if he was okay, if he needed anything; an hour later he said he had to be getting back, but would check in soon. The nurse put a meal down on the table, beside Rose's book of crossword puzzles. Stewart ignored it. She asked if he wanted the TV on; he shook his head.

Stewart refused to eat after that; he told his son he wanted to die. By the time the funeral came around he was too weak to get up. Linda visited a few days later. It started out pleasant. She told him about the turnout and the love in the room, but when he didn't say anything, she started to get worked up. She tried to tell him her mother wouldn't have wanted him moping around like this, and when he still didn't speak she blurted out, "My mom loved life so much and died; it's not fair that you have your life and don't want it." He didn't say anything.

A nurse tried to bully him into eating. She said

there was nothing wrong with him and this wasn't a hotel and he had to start eating and get home so that people who were actually sick could get a bed. Stewart just stared at the ceiling. They forced a feeding tube down his nose. He fought, but by then he was too weak to do much.

He caught a flu and found awareness leaving him. He slept for long stretches, and when he was awake, nothing seemed quite real. At one point, he heard a nurse tell his son that they could keep him alive, but they couldn't make him want to live.

He was aware that he had an infection of some sort and then he was confused to find himself in a different room, not the hospital anymore but not his home. His son was there saying it was okay. Another time consciousness came around and both his boys were there. He heard one of them saying pneumonia, and something about it being for the best; he tried to sit up, panicked, knowing what that meant. But then other memories came back and he relaxed; it was what he wanted.

Acknowledgements

House of Anansi has been my intended publisher since I began writing, and it's an honour to join their list. Thanks to my agent Marilyn Biderman for her support and for arranging the deal; to editor Douglas Richmond for seeing the potential in the collection; to designer Alysia Shewchuk for the striking cover; to publicists Holley Corfield and Rachel Pisani; to managing editor Maria Golikova; and to House of Anansi's publisher Sarah MacLachlan and owner Scott Griffin for putting together an amazing publishing team and list.

Literary magazines and websites are crucial to authors in the early stages of their career; they provide a platform to authors and give them room to develop confidence in their work. My thanks to all the magazines that have published me, especially to Amy Jones for selecting "Low Risk" in the *Puritan*; to Kathryn Mockler at *Joyland* for publishing "Harold"; to the *Maple Tree Literary Supplement* for publishing "Little to Lose"; to *Grain* for publishing "Stewart and Rose"; to the *Lampeter Review* for publishing "What She'd Remember"; to *Cleaver* for publishing "When Things Wear Away Other Things"; and to *Potluck* for publishing "Fun Centre." And a special thanks to Canisia Lubrin, Meaghan Strimas, and Kathryn Kuitenbrouwer for selecting "A Pregnancy" for an honourable mention in the *Humber Literary Review*'s Emerging Writers Fiction Contest — the recognition was a shot in the arm when it was needed.

The Toronto and Ontario Arts Councils provided funding for the writing of this book, without which it would not exist. I thank both organizations dearly.

Many friends and colleagues have helped me with my writing over the years, either by asking how it was going or giving me advice when needed. I thank them all, and would especially like to thank Linda Pruessen, who guided me through the early years of my publishing career, and then the transition to writing, and who also provided copy edits on this book; Janice Zawerbny, who provided advice early on and helped select and improve the stories in this collection; and Jonny Peterson, whose work ethic inspired my own, and who also provided me space in which to work.

And many thanks go to my family. My mom, Edna Melgaard, has been a source of support for my entire life. My partner, Daniella Balabuk, is my first reader. She improved each story before I sent it out, and has saved me much grief by killing my bad ideas before they get out the door. And our kids, Eliot and Charlie. Thank you all.

MICHAEL MELGAARD is a writer and editor based in Toronto. His fiction has appeared in *Joyland*, the *Puritan*, and *Bad Nudes*, among other publications. He has written articles and criticism for the *Millions*, *Torontoist*, and *Canadian Notes & Queries*. *Pallbearing* is his first book.